FANTASTICAL TALES FROM IRISH FOLKLORE

STORIES FROM THE HERO SAGAS AND WONDER-QUESTS

British Library Cataloguing-in-Publication Data
A catalogue record for this book is available from
the British Library

Contents

	Page No.
The Hound of Ulster	1
Standish James O'Grady	
The Wisdom of the King	6
W. B. Yeats	
The Call of Oisin	13
Lady Gregory	
Laughing Stranger	21
James Stephens	
Balor and the Wonder-Smith	28
Ella Young	
The Death of Macha Gold-Hair	45
Dermot O'Byrne	
The Outlaw	56
Joseph O'Neill	
Earth-Bound	64
Dorothy Macardle	
The Women Without Mercy	73
Maurice Walsh	
The Voyage of Maildun	83
P. W. Joyce	
The Heroes of Michan	117
James Joyce	

The Return of Cuchulain.....................122
Eimar O'Duffy
The End of the Rainbow.....................141
Lord Dunsany
Crotty Shinkwin.................................157
A. E. Coppard

<u>Selected Biographies of the Authors</u>

W. B. Yeats.......................................167
James Stephens.................................169
Ella Young..170
Dermot O'Byrne (Arnold Bax)...........171
Joseph O'Neill...................................173
Dorothy Macardle..............................174
P. W. Joyce.......................................175
James Joyce.......................................176
Eimar O'Duffy....................................178
Lord Dunsany.....................................180
A. E. Coppard....................................182

THE HOUND OF ULSTER

Standish James O'Grady

There was much foul play and unfairness practised against Cuculain by the men of Meave, but the Hound of Battle was always their better. Then amongst their number arose one named Lok Mac Favesh.

'Sufficient to me now,' he said, 'is the renown of Cuculain to render him a quarry worthy of my spear. Tomorrow, the host of Meave, released from this check, will cross the Avon Dia, invading the lands of Ulla and in my armoury the head of that brave stripling will be an ornament of my dun, and a boast to my posterity.'

In the morning his squires arrayed him in his battle-dress, his helmet and neck-piece and capacious leathern coat clasped round his breast and mighty waist, and over that they bound his strong breast-plate. To the ford he went like a moving tower, on legs like the trunks of trees, and though corpulent, and past the prime of his youth, nor very quick upon his feet, yet was his strength and power irresistible, which, indeed, all men knew. For, in the previous year, at the feast of Lunasa, held annually in honour to Lu Lamfada, on the plain of Tailteen, on that day which men in later times named the Kalends of August, he had broken in the skull of a bull with a single blow of his strong hand. Seven folds of tanned ox-hide stitched close together, o'er-ran the firm osier work of his shield, and above that was plating of brass two inches thick, and no man in the host of Meave could wield it, but on his arm it was lighter than the bratta which in sudden quarrel a man winds round his left arm, a defence against a knife. It, three brothers of the city of Limerick had made for him, and there was a painted device in the middle.

But, on the other side, came down Cuculain unarmoured, his linen tunic and crimson bratta soiled, and his brooch dulled with rust, his gold tresses tangled, and his countenance hollow and overcast. But harder than steel was his heart in his breast and the men of Meave were astonished and said: 'Is this, indeed, he who played at hurley with us?' for mighty seemed his stature, and terrible his advance, striding through the stunted willows to meet his enemy.

Then his feet splashed in the shallow water of the ford, but suddenly he shrieked, and his spears fell from his hand; for, above the head of Mac Favash he beheld the ghoul that had accompanied him unseen from the south, resting a bearded chin upon skinny knuckles, and it smiled at him. He, Cuculain, stood like one petrified, his eyes starting from their sockets, and his yellow hair stood out from his head. At this Lok Mac Favash advanced, and poising, cast his heavy spear at Cuculain's bare breast, but it erring, went lower towards the left, and passed through the shield at the upper rim, and entered the fleshy part of Cuculain's upper arm.

Dire agony took possession of Cuculain which was his safety, for it restored him to himself. Lok Mac Favash drew to him the spear by the haft, drawing the head out of Cuculain's flesh, but the shoulders held fast in the shield, wherefore he dragged the youth forward struggling and stumbling in the water, as the fisherman draws to land some noble fish, and the blood spurted out and reddened his white tunic and his legs. The men of Meave raised a shout, and that shout was heard in Emain Macha.

Meantime Lok Mac Favash was dragging Cuculain through the ford, and as he did so he laughed at and insulted him.

'Verily ere now, O men of Meave,' he said, 'have I had good sport in fishing. For in the sea below Limerick and in the harbour of Ilaun Ard Nemeth have I drawn into my boat fish, many and great that strongly resisted, and when I brought them into my boat, if troublesome I struck them on the head with a stick. But never till now have I drawn in a fish so vigorous, or that yielded such good sport. Nevertheless, him, too, will I mollify, stroking him down with my little stick.'

Therewith he drew his war-mace, the head alone seventy pounds, all brass, with spikes standing out upon it like the spikes of the sea urchin, and he shook it playfully backwards towards the men of Meave.

Then was there a respite for Cuculain, and very quickly and like the crooked track of the lightning, he drew his sword and smote the spear of Mac Favash just in front of the shield, and struck in twain the strong ashed tree. He recovered quickly the spears which had fallen from him, and with a cry leaped from the ford, strong and vigorous as a salmon springing over a cataract in early summer when he seeks the upper pools, and poising, was about to cast one of his spears at Lok, when, again, the spectre, breathing in his face an icy breath, confronted him, more hellish than before. Yet this time he shrieked not, nor was afraid, for despair and wrath had made him mad. Wherefore altering the direction he hurled at the ghoul the long spear, and it seemed as though it passed through a hollow eye socket.

A horrid cry penetrated the host, whereat the war-steeds and the beasts of burden ran together alarmed, and the whole host shuddered, and men saw some formless thing fall heavily into the ford. But, ere Cuculain could clutch his second spear, Mac Favash bore down upon him like a great ship that throws her billows on both sides from her broad prow, and beat him back into the ford, using both shield and club. Twice in succession he smote with his mighty club the shield of Cuculain, and shattered all the middle of that light shield; Cuculain stepped back nimbly, and again lifted his spear. Once more he cried out with mingled rage and fear, and he stood a moment as if glued to the spot, with his legs close together and working frightfully with his bloody knees.

Then as Lok Mac Favash was advancing to slay him, Cuculain sprang high out of the water, and around his ankles and below the calves of his legs was there coiled three times lapped, the twine of a great eel, blue, with glittering eyes and close-tapped tail. But as he sprang high in the air, Cuculain smote at it with his spear, using it like a staff, striking on the left side, and with a croak like a raven, the horrid thing unwound, and fell into the bloody water.

Cuculain poised once more his spear, and cast it at Lok Mac Favash, but the other held his round shield at an angle, and the spear screeched against the thick brass, grooving it as the ollav grooves the sand with his pen, teaching children to write. Once again Cuculain cried out, trampling wildly with his feet, and the spray went up and concealed the combat from the fierce trampling of the son of Sualtam, and the torn fragments of a strange water-weed floated down the stream from where Cuculain trampled, subduing the third transformation of the spectre.

While he was powerless Lok Mac Favash struck him on the left breast with his spiked club. Now all the middle of Cuculain's shield was broken away, and there was a ragged border all around, and with this border, the weakest part of the shield, he intercepted the blow, but the heavy mace broke through it and fell upon his breast, and the spikes tore his flesh. Then Cuculain staggered. Nevertheless he drew his sword and struck at Lok, but the other

4

caught it on the very boss of the shield, where the brass was four inches thick, and the sword brake and showered about the stream.

Cuculain looked for a moment to the wide heaven and the sun, for it was blazing noon, and his lips moved, and, swerving swiftly to the right, he stooped. Now, a row of great pebbles crossed the ford, the work of some ancient king, and in a crescent-shaped line traversed the water and the dry land on each side, in order that, even in times of flood, there might be a passage for travellers, and below this was a chariot-ford where the heroes fought. Dropping the fragments of his shield, he laid his hands on the largest of these, smooth and white on the top, worn by many feet, but black and mossy upon the sides. A stone that two strong navvies, such as men are now, could with difficulty roll to the shore, using cow-bars, but Cuculain raised it without difficulty. As a boy, eager to get at the sweet kernel, with ease lifts the strong-shelled fruit of the palm tree, and smashes it against the flagged basement, so Cuculain raised on high above his head the mighty pebble, standing with legs apart in the ford, and dashed it on the centre of the huge shield of Lok Mac Favish.

The great stone smashed through the broad shield of Lok, and smote him below the breast, and bore him to the ground, falling upon him, as one who wrestles with his enemy and falls with him to the ground, and it crushed him down under the water. But it wanted not water to slay him, for his body was broken from the impulse of the heavy missile. Cuculain seized the spear-tree of Lok's spear which was eddying around the place, and leant upon it, panting red all over as though he had ascended out of a bath of blood.

Then he drew himself together and sat down on one of the great pebbles, bowing his head between his hands, and vomited much blood into the stream. After which he rose and walked to the other shore, staggering as he went, and steadying his steps with the spear, and passed in between the willows. And the whole host of Meave was silent, and every eye watched him, warriors craning forward with raised hands, watching eagerly if he would fall. As when a sportsman and his beaters watch eagerly the flight of a bird which they deem is wounded, and one says he will fall, and another not, so the great host of Meave watched Cuculain as he went back, till the trees concealed him.

THE WISDOM OF THE KING

W. B. Yeats

*   *   *

The High-Queen of the Island of Woods had died in childbirth, and her child was put to nurse with a woman who lived in a hut of mud and wicker, within the border of the wood. One night the woman sat rocking the cradle, and pondering over the beauty of the child, and praying that the gods might grant him wisdom equal to his beauty. There came a knock at the door, and she got up, not a little wondering, for the nearest neighbours were in the dun of the High-King a mile away; and the night was now late. 'Who is knocking?' she cried, and a thin voice answered, 'Open! for I am a crone of the grey hawk, and I come from the darkness of the great wood.' In terror she drew back the bolt, and a grey-clad woman, of a great age, and of a height more than human, came in and stood by the head of the cradle. The nurse shrank back against the wall, unable to take her eyes from the woman, for she saw by the gleaming of the firelight that the feathers of the grey hawk were upon her head instead of hair. But the child slept, and the fire danced, for the one was too ignorant and the other too full of gaiety to know what a dreadful being stood there. 'Open!' cried another voice, 'for I am a crone of the grey hawk, and I watch over his nest in the darkness of the great wood.' The nurse opened the door again, though her fingers could scarce hold the bolts for trembling, and another grey woman, not less old than the other, and with like feathers instead of hair, came in and stood by the first. In a little, came a third grey woman, and after her a fourth, and then another and another and another, until the hut was full of their immense bodies. They stood a long time in perfect silence and stillness, for they were of those whom the dropping of the sand has never troubled, but at last one muttered in a low thin voice: 'Sisters, I knew him far away by the redness of his heart under his silver skin'; and then another spoke: 'Sisters, I knew him because his heart fluttered like a bird under a net of silver cords'; and then another took up the word: 'Sisters, I knew him because his heart sang like a bird that is happy in a silver cage.'

And after that they sang together, those who were nearest rocking the cradle with long wrinkled fingers; and their voices were now tender and caressing, now like the wind blowing in the great wood, and this was their song:

> Out of sight is out of mind:
> Long have man and woman-kind,
> Heavy of will and light of mood,
> Taken away our wheaten food,
> Taken away our Altar stone;

Hail and rain and thunder alone,
And red hearts we turn to grey,
Are true till Time gutter away.

When the song had died out, the crone who had first spoken, said: 'We have nothing more to do but to mix a drop of our blood into his blood.' And she scratched her arm with the sharp point of a spindle, which she had made the nurse bring to her, and let a drop of blood, grey as the mist, fall upon the lips of the child; and passed out into the darkness. Then the others passed out in silence one by one; and all the while the child had not opened his pink eyelids or the fire ceased to dance, for the one was too ignorant and the other too full of gaiety to know what great beings had bent over the cradle.

When the crones were gone, the nurse came to her courage again, and hurried to the dun of the High-King, and cried out in the midst of the assembly hall that the Sidhe, whether for good or evil she knew not, had bent over the child that night; and the king and his poets and men of law, and his huntsmen, and his cooks, and his chief warriors went with her to the hut and gathered about the cradle, and were as noisy as magpies, and the child sat up and looked at them.

Two years passed over, and the king died fighting against the Fer Bolg; and the poets and the men of law ruled in the name of the child, but looked to see him become the master himself before long, for no one had seen so wise a child, and tales of his endless questions about the household of the gods and the making of the world went hither and thither among the wicker houses of the poor. Everything had been well but for a miracle that began to trouble all men; and all women, who, indeed, talked of it without ceasing. The feathers of the grey hawk had begun to grow in the child's hair, and though his nurse cut them continually, in but a little while they would be more numerous than ever. This had not been a matter of great moment, for miracles were a little thing in those days, but for an ancient law of Eri that none who had any blemish of body could sit upon the throne; and as a grey hawk was a wild thing of the air which had never sat at the board, or listened to the songs of the poets in the light of the fire, it was not possible to think of one in whose hair its feathers grew as other than marred and blasted; nor could the people separate from their admiration of the wisdom that grew in him a horror as at one of unhuman blood.

Yet all were resolved that he should reign, for they had suffered much from foolish kings and their own disorders, and moreover they desired to watch out the spectacle of his days; and no one had any other fear but that his great wisdom might bid him obey the law, and call some other, who had but a common mind, to reign in his stead.

When the child was seven years old the poets and the men of law were called together by the chief poet, and all these matters weighed and considered. The child had already seen that those about him had hair only, and, though they had told him that they too had had feathers but had lost them because of a sin committed by their forefathers, they knew that he would learn the truth when he began to wander into the country round about. After much consideration they decreed a new law commanding every one upon pain of death to mingle artificially the feathers of the grey hawk into his hair; and they sent men with nets and slings and bows into the countries round about to gather a sufficiency of feathers. They decreed also that any who told the truth to the child should be flung from a cliff into the sea.

The years passed, and the child grew from childhood into boyhood and from boyhood into manhood, and from being curious about all things he became busy with strange and subtle thoughts which came to him in dreams, and with distinctions between things long held the same and with the resemblance of things long held different. Multitudes came from other lands to see him and to ask his counsel, but there were guards set at the frontiers, who compelled all that came to wear the feathers of the grey hawk in their hair.

While they listened to him his words seemed to make all darkness light and filled their hearts like music; but, alas, when they returned to their own lands his words seemed far off, and what they could remember too strange and subtle to help them to live out their hasty days. A number indeed did live differently afterwards, but their new life was less excellent than the old: some among them had long served a good cause, but when they heard him praise it and their labour, they returned to their own lands to find what they had loved less lovable and their arm lighter in the battle, for he had taught them how little a hair divides the false and true; others, again, who had served no cause, but wrought in peace the welfare of their own households, when he had expounded the meaning of their purpose, found their bones softer and their will less ready for toil, for he had shown them greater purposes; and numbers of the young, when they had heard him upon all these things, remembered certain words that became like a fire in their hearts, and made all kindly joys and traffic between man and man as nothing, and went different ways, but all into vague regret.

When any asked him concerning the common things of life; disputes about the mear of a territory, or about the straying of cattle, or about the penalty of blood; he would turn to those nearest him for advice; but this was held to be from courtesy, for none knew that these matters were hidden from him by thoughts and dreams that filled his mind like the marching and counter-marching of armies. Far less could any know that his heart wandered lost amid throngs of overcoming thoughts and dreams, shuddering at its own consuming solitude.

Among those who came to look at him and to listen to him was the daughter of a little king who lived a great way off; and when he saw her he loved, for she was beautiful, with a strange and pale beauty unlike the women of his land; but Dana, the great mother, had decreed her a heart that was but as the heart of others, and when she considered the mystery of the hawk feathers she was troubled with a great horror. He called her to him when the assembly was over and told her of her beauty, and praised her simply and frankly as though she were a fable of the bards; and he asked her humbly to give him her love, for he was only subtle in his dreams. Overwhelmed with his greatness, she half consented, and yet half refused, for she longed to marry some warrior who could carry her over a mountain in his arms.

Day by day the king gave her gifts; cups with ears of gold and findrinny wrought by the craftsmen of distant lands; cloth from over sea, which, though woven with curious figures, seemed to her less beautiful than the bright cloth of her own country; and still she was ever between a smile and a frown; between yielding and withholding. He laid down his wisdom at her feet, and told how the heroes when they die return to the world and begin their labour anew; how the kind and mirthful Men of Dea drove out the huge and gloomy and misshapen People from Under the Sea;

and a multitude of things that even the Sidhe have forgotten, either because they happened so long ago or because they have not time to think of them; and still she half refused, and still he hoped, because he could not believe that a beauty so much like wisdom could hide a common heart.

There was a tall young man in the dun who had yellow hair, and was skilled in wrestling and in the training of horses; and one day when the king walked in the orchard, which was between the foss and the forest, he heard his voice among the salley bushes which hid the waters of the foss.

'My blossom,' it said, 'I hate them for making you weave these dingy feathers into your beautiful hair, and all that the bird of prey upon the throne may sleep easy o' nights'; and then the low, musical voice he loved answered: 'My hair is not beautiful like yours; and now that I have plucked the feathers out of your hair I will put my hands through it, thus, and thus, and thus; for it casts no shadow of terror and darkness upon my heart.'

Then the king remembered many things that he had forgotten without understanding them, doubtful words of his poets and his men of law, doubts that he had reasoned away, his own continual solitude; and he called to the lovers in a trembling voice. They came from among the salley bushes and threw themselves at his feet and prayed for pardon, and he stooped down and plucked the feathers out of the hair of the woman and then turned away towards the dun without a word. He strode into the hall of assembly, and having gathered his poets and his men of law about him, stood upon the daïs and spoke in a loud, clear voice:

'Men of law, why did you make me sin against the laws of Eri? Men of verse, why did you make me sin against the secrecy of wisdom, for law was made by man for the welfare of man, but wisdom the gods have made, and no man shall live by its light, for it and the hail and the rain and the thunder follow a way that is deadly to mortal things? Men of law and men of verse, live according to your kind, and call Eocha of the Hasty Mind to reign over you, for I set out to find my kindred.'

He then came down among them, and drew out of the hair of first one and then another the feathers of the grey hawk, and, having scattered them over the rushes upon the floor, passed out, and none dared to follow him, for his eyes gleamed like the eyes of the birds of prey; and no man saw him again or heard his voice.

Some believed that he found his eternal abode among the demons, and some that he dwelt henceforth with the dark and dreadful goddesses, who sit all night about the pools in the forest watching the constellations rising and setting in those desolate mirrors.

THE CALL OF OISIN

Lady Gregory

*   *   *

One misty morning, what were left of the Fianna were gathered together to Finn, and it is sorrowful and downhearted they were after the loss of so many of their comrades.

And they went hunting near the borders of Loch Lein, where the bushes were in blossom and the birds were singing; and they were waking up the deer that were as joyful as the leaves of a tree in summer-time.

And it was not long till they saw coming towards them from the west a beautiful young woman, riding on a very fast slender white horse. A queen's crown she had on her head, and a dark cloak of silk down to the ground, having stars of red gold on it; and her eyes were blue and as clear as the dew on the grass, and a gold ring hanging down from every golden lock of her hair; and her cheeks redder than the rose, and her skin whiter than the swan upon the wave, and her lips as sweet as honey that is mixed through red wine.

And in her hand she was holding a bridle having a golden bit, and there was a saddle worked with red gold under her. And as to the horse, he had a wide smooth cloak over him, and a silver crown on the back of his head, and he was shod with shining gold.

She came to where Finn was, and she spoke with a very kind, gentle voice, and she said: 'It is long my journey was, King of the Fianna.' And Finn asked who was she, and what was her country and the cause of her coming. 'Niamh of the Golden Head is my name,' she said; 'and I have a name beyond all the women of the world, for I am the daughter of the King of the Country of the Young.' 'What was it brought you to us from over the sea, Queen?' said Finn then. 'Is it that your husband is gone from you, or what is the trouble that is on you?' 'My husband is not gone from me,' she said, 'for I never went yet to any man. But O King of the Fianna,' she said, 'I have given my love and my affection to your own son, Oisin of the strong hands.' 'Why did you give your love to him beyond all the troops of high princes that are under the sun?' said Finn. 'It was by reason of his great name, and of the report I heard of his bravery and of his comeliness,' she said. 'And though there is many a king's son and high prince gave me his love, I never consented to any till I set my love on Oisin.'

When Oisin heard what she was saying, there was not a limb of his body that was not in love with beautiful Niamh; and he took her hand in his hand, and he said: 'A true welcome before you to this country, young queen. It is you are the shining one,' he said; 'it is you are the nicest and the comeliest; it is you are better to me than any other woman; it is you are my star and my choice beyond the women of the entire world.' 'I put on you the bonds of a true hero,' said Niamh then, 'you to come away with me now to the Country of the Young.' And it is what she said:

'It is the country is most delightful of all that are under the sun;

14

the trees are stooping down with fruit and with leaves and with blossom.

'Honey and wine are plentiful there, and everything the eye has ever seen; no wasting will come on you with the wasting away of time; you will never see death or lessening.

'You will get feasts, playing and drinking; you will get sweet music on the strings; you will get silver and gold and many jewels.

'You will get, and no lie in it, a hundred swords; a hundred cloaks of the dearest silk; a hundred horses, the quickest in battle; a hundred willing hounds.

'You will get the royal crown of the King of the Young that he never gave to any one under the sun. It will be a shelter to you night and day in every rough fight and in every battle.

'You will get a right suit of armour; a sword, goldhilted, apt for striking; no one that ever saw it got away alive from it.

'A hundred coats of armour and shirts of satin; a hundred cows and a hundred calves; a hundred sheep having golden fleeces; a hundred jewels that are not of this world.

'A hundred glad young girls shining like the sun, their voices sweeter than the music of birds; a hundred armed men strong in battle, apt at feats, waiting on you, if you will come with me to the Country of the Young.

'You will get everything I have said to you, and delights beyond them, that I have no leave to tell; you will get beauty, strength and power, and I myself will be with you as a wife.'

And after she had made that song, Oisin said: 'O pleasant golden-haired queen, you are my choice beyond the women of the world; and I will go with you willingly,' he said.

And with that he kissed Finn his father and bade him farewell, and he bade farewell to the rest of the Fianna, and he went up then on the horse with Niamh.

And the horse set out gladly, and when he came to the strand he shook himself and he neighed three times, and then he made for the sea. And when Finn and the Fianna saw Oisin facing the wide sea, they gave three great sorrowful shouts. And as to Finn, he said: 'It is my grief to see you going from me; and I am without a hope,' he said, 'ever to see you coming back to me again.'

*   *   *

It was a long time after he was brought away by Niamh that Oisin came back again to Ireland. Some say it was hundreds of years he was in the Country of the Young, and some say it was thousands of years he was in it; but whatever time it was, it seemed short to him.

And whatever happened him through the time he was away, it is a withered old man he was found after coming back to Ireland, and his white horse going away from him, and he lying on the ground.

And it was St Patrick had power at that time, and it was to him Oisin was brought; and he kept him in his house, and used to be teaching him and questioning him. And Oisin was no way pleased with the way Ireland was then, but he used to be talking of the old times, and fretting after the Fianna.

And Patrick bade him to tell what happened him the time he left Finn and the Fianna and went away with Niamh. And it is the story Oisin told: 'The time I went away with golden-haired Niamh, we turned our backs to the land, and our faces westward, and the sea was going away before us, and filling up in waves after us. And we saw wonderful things on our journey,' he said, 'cities and courts and duns and lime-white houses, and shining sunny-houses and palaces. And one time we saw beside us a hornless deer running hard, and an eager white red-eared hound following after it. And another time we saw a young girl on a horse and having a golden apple in her right hand, and she going over the tops of the waves; and there was following after her a young man riding a white horse, and having a crimson cloak and a gold-hilted sword in his right hand.'

'Follow on with your story, pleasant Oisin,' said Patrick, 'for you did not tell us yet what was the country you went to.'

'The Country of the Young, the Country of Victory, it was,' said Oisin. 'And O Patrick,' he said, 'there is no lie in that name; and if there are grandeurs in your Heaven the same as there are there, I would give my friendship to God.

'We turned our backs then to the dun,' he said, 'and the horse under us was quicker than the spring wind on the backs of the mountains. And it was not long till the sky darkened, and the wind rose in every part, and the sea was as if on fire, and there was nothing to be seen of the sun.

'But after we were looking at the clouds and the stars for a while

the wind went down, and the storm, and the sun brightened. And
we saw before us a very delightful country under full blossom, and
smooth plains in it, and a king's dun that was very grand, and that
had every colour in it, and sunny-houses beside it, and palaces of
shining stones, made by skilled men. And we saw coming out to
meet us three fifties of armed men, very lively and handsome.
And I asked Niamh was this the Country of the Young, and she
said it was. "And indeed, Oisin," she said, "I told you no lie about
it, and you will see all I promised you before you for ever."

'And there came out after that a hundred beautiful young girls,
having cloaks of silk worked with gold, and they gave me a welcome to their own country. And after that there came a great
shining army, and with it a strong beautiful king, having a shirt of
yellow silk and a golden cloak over it, and a very bright crown on
his head. And there was following after him a young queen, and
fifty young girls along with her.

'And when all were come to the one spot, the king took me by
the hand, and he said out before them all: "A hundred thousand
welcomes before you, Oisin, son of Finn. And as to this country
you are come to," he said, "I will tell you news of it without a
lie. It is long and lasting your life will be in it, and you yourself
will be young for ever. And there is no delight the heart ever
thought of," he said, "but it is here against your coming. And you
can believe my words, Oisin," he said, "for I myself am the King
of the Country of the Young, and this is its comely queen, and it
was golden-headed Niamh our daughter that went over the sea
looking for you to be her husband for ever." I gave thanks to him
then, and I stooped myself down before the queen, and we went
forward to the royal house, and all the high nobles came out to
meet us, both men and women, and there was a great feast made
there through the length of ten days and ten nights.

'And that is the way I married Niamh of the Golden Hair, and
that is the way I went to the Country of the Young, although it is
sorrowful to me to be telling it now, O Patrick from Rome,' said
Oisin.

'Follow on with your story, Oisin of the destroying arms,' said
Patrick, 'and tell me what way did you leave the Country of the
Young, for it is long to me till I hear that; and tell us now had
you any children by Niamh, and was it long you were in that
place.'

'Three beautiful children I had by Niamh,' said Oisin, 'two young sons and a comely daughter. And Niamh gave the two sons the name of Finn and of Osgar, and the name I gave to the daughter was The Flower.

'And I did not feel the time passing, and it was a long time I stopped there,' he said, 'till the desire came on me to see Finn and my comrades again. And I asked leave of the king and of Niamh to go back to Ireland. "You will get leave from me," said Niamh; "but for all that," she said, "it is bad news you are giving me, for I am in dread you will never come back here again through the length of your days." But I bade her have no fear, since the white horse would bring me safe back again from Ireland. "Bear this in mind, Oisin," she said then, "if you once get off the horse while you are away, or if you once put your foot to ground, you will never come back here again. And O Oisin,' she said, 'I tell it to you now for the third time, if you once get down from the horse, you will be an old man, blind and withered, without liveliness, without mirth, without running, without leaping. And it is a grief to me, Oisin,' she said, 'you ever to go back to green Ireland; and it is not now as it used to be, and you will not see Finn and his people, for there is not now in the whole of Ireland but a Father of Orders and armies of saints; and here is my kiss for you, pleasant Oisin,' she said, 'for you will never come back any more to the Country of the Young.'

'And that is my story, Patrick, and I have told you no lie in it,' said Oisin. 'And O Patrick,' he said, 'if I was the same the day I came here as I was that day, I would have made an end of all your clerks, and there would not be a head left on a neck after me.'

'Go on with your story,' said Patrick, 'and you will get the same good treatment from me you got from Finn, for the sound of your voice is pleasing to me.'

So Oisin went on with his story, and it is what he said: 'I have nothing to tell of my journey till I came back into green Ireland, and I looked about me then on all sides, but there were no tidings to be got of Finn. And it was not long till I saw a great troop of riders, men and women, coming towards me from the west. And when they came near they wished me good health; and there was wonder on them all when they looked at me, seeing me so unlike themselves, and so big and so tall.

'I asked them then did they hear if Finn was still living, or any other one of the Fianna, or what had happened them. 'We often heard of Finn that lived long ago,' said they, 'and that there never was his equal for strength or bravery or a great name; and there is many a book written down,' they said, 'by the sweet poets of the Gael, about his doings and the doings of the Fianna, and it would be hard for us to tell you all of them. And we heard Finn had a son,' they said, 'that was beautiful and shining, and that there came a young girl looking for him, and he went away with her to the Country of the Young.'

'And when I knew by their talk that Finn was not living or any of the Fianna, it is downhearted I was, and tired, and very sorrowful after them. And I made no delay, but I turned my face and went on to Almhuin of Leinster. And there was great wonder on me when I came there to see no sign at all of Finn's great dun, and his great hall, and nothing in the place where it was but weeds and nettles.'

And there was grief on Oisin then, and he said: 'Och, Patrick! Och, ochone, my grief! It is a bad journey that was to me; and to be without tidings of Finn or the Fianna has left me under pain through my lifetime.'

'Leave off fretting, Oisin,' said Patrick, 'and shed your tears to the God of grace. Finn and the Fianna are slack enough now, and they will get no help for ever.' 'It is a great pity that would be,' said Oisin, 'Finn to be in pain for ever; and who was it gained the victory over him, when his own hand had made an end of so many a hard fighter?'

'It is God gained the victory over Finn,' said Patrick, 'and not the strong hand of an enemy; and as to the Fianna, they are condemned to hell along with him, and tormented for ever.'

'O Patrick,' said Oisin, 'show me the place where Finn and his people are, and there is not a hell or a heaven there but I will put it down. And if Osgar, my own son, is there,' he said, 'the hero that was bravest in heavy battles, there is not in hell or in the Heaven of God a troop so great that he could not destroy it.'

'Let us leave off quarrelling on each side now,' said Patrick; 'and go on, Oisin, with your story. What happened you after you knew the Fianna to be at an end?'

'I will tell you that, Patrick,' said Oisin. 'I was turning to go away, and I saw the stone trough that the Fianna used to be putting their hands in, and it full of water. And when I saw it I had such a wish and such a feeling for it that I forgot what I was told, and I got off the horse. And in the minute all the years came on me, and I was lying on the ground, and the horse took fright and went away and left me there, an old man, weak and spent, without sight, without shape, without comeliness, without strength or understanding, without respect.

'There, Patrick, is my story for you now,' said Oisin, 'and no lie in it, of all that happened me going away and coming back again from the Country of the Young.'

LAUGHING STRANGER

James Stephens

*   *   *

In the days of long ago and the times that have disappeared for
ever, there was one Fiachna Finn the son of Baltan, the son of
Murchertach, the son of Muredach, the son of Eogan, the son

of Neill. He went from his own country when he was young, for he wished to see the land of Lochlann, and he wished that he would be welcomed by the king of that country, for Fiachna's father and Eolgarg's father had done deeds in common and were obliged to each other. He was welcomed, and he stayed at the Court of Lochlann in great ease and in the midst of pleasures.

It then happened that Eolgarg Mor fell sick and the doctors could not cure him. They sent for other doctors, but they could not cure him, nor could any one say what he was suffering from, beyond that he was wasting visibly before their eyes, and would certainly become a shadow and disappear in air unless he was healed and fattened and made visible.

They sent for more distant doctors, and then for others more distant still, and at last they found a man who claimed that he could make a cure if the king were supplied with the medicine which he would order.

'What medicine is that?' said they all.

'This is the medicine,' said the doctor. 'Find a perfectly white cow with red ears, and boil it down in the lump, and if the king drinks that rendering he will recover.'

Before he had well said it messengers were going from the palace in all directions looking for such a cow. They found lots of cows which were nearly like what they wanted, but it was only by chance that they came on the cow which would do the work, and that beast belonged to the most notorious and malicious and cantankerous female in Lochlann, the Black Hag.

Now the Black Hag was not only those things that have been said; she was whiskered and warty and one-eyed and obstreperous, and she was notorious and ill-favoured in other ways also.

They offered her a cow in the place of her own cow, but she refused to give it. Then they offered a cow for each leg of her cow, but she would not accept that offer unless Fiachna went bail for the payment. He agreed to do so, and they drove the beast away.

On the return journey he was met by messengers who brought news from Ireland. They said that the King of Ulster was dead, and that he, Fiachna Finn, had been elected king in the dead king's place. He at once took ship for Ireland, and found that all he had been told was true, and he took up the government of Ulster.

A year passed, and one day as he was sitting at judgment there came a great noise from without, and this noise was so persistent that the people and suitors were scandalised, and Fiachna at last ordered that the noisy person should be brought before him to be judged. It was done, and to his surprise the person turned out to be the Black Hag.

She blamed him in the court before his people and complained that he had taken away her cow, and that she had not been paid the four cows he had gone bail for, and she demanded judgment from him and justice.

'If you will consider it to be justice, I will give you twenty cows myself,' said Fiachna.

'I will not take all the cows in Ulster,' she screamed.

'Pronounce judgment yourself,' said the king, 'and if I can do what you demand I will do it.' For he did not like to be in the wrong, and he did not wish that any person should have an unsatisfied claim upon him.

The Black Hag then pronounced judgment, and the king had to fulfil it.

'I have come,' said she, 'from the east to the west; you must come from the west to the east and make war for me, and revenge me on the King of Lochlann.'

Fiachna had to do as she demanded, and, although it was with a heavy heart, he set out in three days' time for Lochlann, and he brought with him ten battalions.

He sent messengers before him to Big Eolgarg warning him of his coming, of his intention, and of the number of troops he was bringing; and when he landed Eolgarg met him with an equal force, and they fought together.

In the first battle three hundred of the men of Lochlann were killed, but in the next battle Eolgarg Mor did not fight fair, for he let some venomous sheep out of a tent, and these attacked the men of Ulster and killed nine hundred of them.

So vast was the slaughter made by these sheep and so great the terror they caused, that no one could stand before them, but by great good luck there was a wood at hand, and the men of Ulster, warriors and princes and charioteers, were forced to climb up the trees, and they roosted among the branches like great birds, while the venomous sheep ranged below, bleating terribly and tearing up the ground.

Fiachna Finn was also sitting in a tree, very high up, and he was disconsolate. 'We are disgraced!' said he.

'It is very lucky,' said the man in the branch below, 'that a sheep cannot climb a tree.'

'We are disgraced for ever!' said the King of Ulster.

'If those sheep learn how to climb, we are undone surely,' said the man below.

'I will go down and fight the sheep,' said Fiachna.

But the others would not let the king go.

'It is not right,' they said, 'that you should fight sheep.'

'Some one must fight them,' said Fiachna Finn, 'but no more of my men shall die until I fight myself; for if I am fated to die, I will die and I cannot escape it, and if it is the sheep's fate to die, then die they will; for there is no man can avoid destiny, and there is no sheep can dodge it either.'

'Praise be to God!' said the warrior that was higher up.

'Amen!' said the man who was higher than he, and the rest of the warriors wished good luck to the king.

He started then to climb down the tree with a heavy heart, but while he hung from the last branch and was about to let go, he noticed a tall warrior walking towards him. The king pulled himself up on the branch again and sat dangle-legged on it to see what the warrior would do.

The stranger was a very tall man, dressed in a green cloak with a silver brooch at the shoulder. He had a golden band about his hair and golden sandals on his feet, and he was laughing heartily at the plight of the men of Ireland.

'It is not nice of you to laugh at us,' said Fiachna Finn.

'Who could help laughing at a king hunkering on a branch and his army roosting around like hens?' said the stranger.

'Nevertheless,' the king replied, 'it would be courteous of you not to laugh at misfortune.'

'We laugh when we can,' commented the stranger, 'and are thankful for the chance.'

'You may come up into the tree,' said Fiachna, 'for I perceive that you are a mannerly person, and I see that some of the venomous sheep are charging in this direction. I would rather protect you,' he continued, 'than see you killed; for,' said he lamentably, 'I am getting down now to fight the sheep.'

'They will not hurt me,' said the stranger.

'Who are you?' the king asked.

'I am Manannan, the son of Lir.'

Fiachna knew then that the stranger could not be hurt.

'What will you give me if I deliver you from the sheep?' asked Manannan.

'I will give you anything you ask, if I have that thing.'

'I ask the rights of your crown and of your household for one day.'

Fiachna's breath was taken away by that request, and he took a little time to compose himself, then he said mildly:

'I will not have one man of Ireland killed if I can save him. All that I have they give me, all that I have I give to them, and if I must give this also, then I will give this, although it would be easier for me to give my life.'

'That is agreed,' said Manannan.

He had something wrapped in a fold of his cloak, and he unwrapped and produced this thing.

It was a dog.

Now if the sheep were venomous, this dog was more venomous still, for it was fearful to look at. In body it was not large, but its head was of a great size, and the mouth that was shaped in that head was able to open like the lid of a pot. It was not teeth that were in that head, but hooks and fangs and prongs. Dreadful was that mouth to look at, terrible to look into, woeful to think about; and from it, or from the broad, loose nose that waggled above it, there came a sound which no word of man could describe, for it was not a snarl, nor was it a howl, although it was both of these.

It was neither a growl nor a grunt, although it was both of these; it was not a yowl nor a groan, although it was both of these: for it was one sound made up of these sounds, and there was in it, too, a whine and a yelp, and a long-drawn snoring noise, and a deep purring noise, and a noise that was like the squeal of a rusty hinge, and there were other noises in it also.

'The gods be praised!' said the man who was in the branch above the king.

'What for this time?' said the king.

25

'Because that dog cannot climb a tree,' said the man.

And a man on a branch yet above him groaned out, 'Amen!'

'There is nothing to frighten sheep like a dog,' said Manannan, 'and there is nothing to frighten these sheep like this dog.'

He put the dog on the ground then.

'Little dogeen, little treasure,' he said, 'go and kill the sheep.'

And when he said that the dog put an addition and an addendum on to the noise he had been making before, so that the men of Ireland stuck their fingers into their ears and turned the whites of their eyes upwards, and nearly fell off their branches with the fear and the fright which that sound put into them.

It did not take the dog long to do what he had been ordered. He went forward, at first, with a slow waddle, and as the venomous sheep came to meet him in bounces, he then went to meet them in wriggles; so that in a while he went so fast that you could see nothing of him but a head and a wriggle. He dealt with the sheep in this way, a jump and a chop for each, and he never missed his jump and he never missed his chop. When he got his grip he swung round on it as if it was a hinge. The swing began with the chop, and it ended with the bit loose and the sheep giving its last kick. At the end of ten minutes all the sheep were lying on the ground, and the same bit was out of every sheep, and every sheep was dead.

'You can come down now,' said Manannan.

'That dog can't climb a tree,' said the man in the branch above the king warningly.

'Praise be to the gods!' said the man who was above him.

'Amen!' said the warrior who was higher up than that.

And the man in the next tree said: 'Don't move a hand or a foot until the dog chokes himself to death on the dead meat.'

The dog did not eat a bit of the meat. He trotted to his master, and Manannan took him up and wrapped him in his cloak.

'Now you can come down,' said he.

'I wish that dog was dead,' said the king.

But he swung himself out of the tree all the same, for he did not wish to seem frightened before Manannan.

'You can go now and beat the men of Lochlann,' said Manannan. 'You will be King of Lochlann before nightfall.'

'I wouldn't mind that,' said the king.

'It's no threat,' said Manannan.

The son of Lir turned then and went away in the direction of Ireland to take up his one-day rights, and Fiachna continued his battle with the Lochlannachs.

He beat them before nightfall, and by that victory he became King of Lochlann and King of the Saxons and the Britons.

He gave the Black Hag seven castles with their territories, and he gave her one hundred of every sort of cattle that he had captured. She was satisfied.

Then he went back to Ireland, and after he had been there for some time his wife gave birth to a son.

BALOR AND THE WONDER-SMITH

Ella Young

The oak-wood in the Gap of the Dragon was Summer-heavy: its branches held a murmurous stillness. Sunshine drowsed in it. The road through the Gap was sun-parched. The Son of the Gubbaun sat by the edge of the wood. He was cutting the ogham of a poem on a stave of holly, and he crooned the verse as he worked. Suddenly a strangling blackness clutched him, a breath as of Winter chilled him. The holly stave dropped from his hands. He rose stumblingly.

The road through the Gap was filled with strange creatures: monstrous uncouth animals straddled on it; dwarfs and giants, men that seemed deformed, crowded on it. They were cloaked and hooded. The two that stood nearest to the Son of the Gubbaun had robes that were stiff with gems. Their faces were masked in gold. Their towering headdresses glittered.

'We are come,' cried they, 'from the Court of Balor of the Mighty Blows, King of the Fomor. A fame and a rumour of the Gubbaun Saor, the Wonder-Smith, has come over the Black Waters into the country of Balor: it has stirred the mind of the king. He would have the Gubbaun build him a dun, a bulk, a rooted vastness that will be a weight upon the earth, a piled-up mountainous strength. To you, O Wonder-Smith, our king sends gifts and tokens. He will not stint the reward.'

'You do not speak with the Gubbaun Saor. I am his Son.'

'O Son of the Gubbaun Saor entreat your father for us: of you, too, a rumour has come. Our king be-speaks your countenance and help. Behold the gifts and tokens of Balor!'

Eight slaves blacker than charred wood led forward a pack-bearing beast: a beast to wonder at. He had horns that a bull could not carry: his hide was striped and barred like a tiger's, and a bush of hair, curling in twists, spread on his shoulders. He knelt heavily, and the slaves uncovered a world of riches before the Son of the Gubbaun Saor. They showed him cloths woven of gold and find-ruiny with patterned dragons coiling in their folds; drinking-cups crusted with gems; daggers hilted with narwhale tooth. The Son of the Gubbaun fingered emeralds as big as the egg of a gull and greener than a field of grass. Deep azurecoloured sapphires slipped through his hands; topazes that were rose-red; rubies like blood: stones very great and precious.

'Choose arles and earnest-money from amongst these,' said Balor's messengers, 'and at the Black Waters Balor's folk will await you.'

The Son of the Gubbaun chose a ruby, and a stone in which diver colours were spilt. His mind was tangled in the stones for a moment, and when he lifted up his eyes the road was emptiness. The gorgeous train, the fantastic beasts, the lords that had peacocked it, were gone! The sun was hot on his face.

It was with speed and with promptitude and with a fine energy of running that he set out for the house of the Gubbaun. The Gubbaun himself was on the threshold.

'Wonder-Smith,' cried the Son, 'I have seen a vision though it is not the Eve of Samhain. I have talked with lords from a far country. I have a token for you.'

He showed the precious stones and told what had befallen.

'I have worked for many kings,' said the Gubbaun, 'and was ever the kingliest myself. Balor is a blackener of the earth. He has one eye in the centre of his forehead that can devastate walled cities and blast a country-side. His breath freezes the sea-furrows. Why should I go to the country of Balor?'

'A strange land must Balor's country be,' said the Son, 'a land of chasms and deserts and icy fastnesses: the beasts of it are not like the beasts of the green earth: the skies have desolate lights in them: the lords of it hide their faces. Strange happenings wait for us in Balor's country. Are you not tired of the roads we know? Is not triumph sweet in an alien land? Let us go to the country of Balor I entreat you.'

'Because the green pastures have given you strength and lusti-hood,' said the Gubbaun, 'the desert delights you, and the road that dips under the sky-line entices your feet. But since it is so, let us start for the country of Balor with the rising of the sun tomorrow. There is no end to the hunger of the mind.'

Before the rising of the sun they rose. The Gubbaun took a gift to the Well of the Hazels. He cut a little rod from the Hazel Tree. He bathed his forehead. But the Son, too eager to start, did none of these things: he was choosing a travelling-cloak.

'May every day delight you till I come back bringing a gift from the Fomor!' he cried to Aunya, and ran out.

The Gubbaun Saor followed.

They had not gone far when the Gubbaun said: 'Son, shorten the road for me.'

'Put a shape of running on yourself,' said the Son, 'and your own two feet will shorten it.'

'Is that all the road-wisdom you have?' said the Gubbaun.

'It is,' said the Son.

'We may as well go back,' said the Gubbaun, 'It's little help you would be to me in Balor's country.'

Home they went. The Gubbaun shut himself up with his engines and secret contrivances, but the Son sat down by the hearth, and the Hound laid a head on his knee. The Gubbaun's Son caressed the Hound and he made a little rann for him. He said:

> *'Hound*
> *My heart's delight*
> *Moon-white*
> *Sun-bright*
> *Hound from Under-the-Sea*
> *You left a King*
> *To follow me.*

And O Hound, and O Hound,' said the Gubbaun Saor's Son, 'if my wits were as nimble as your feet I wouldn't be sitting here now.'

'The Hound drank at dawn from the Sacred Well,' said Aunya, 'have you returned for a draught?'

'It was a misfortune that brought me back,' said the Son, 'My father bade me to shorten the road for him. I told him to put a shape of running on himself. He would have none of it. And since I am not a winged demon of the storm, or a gray hawk of the cliffs, I could think only of the swiftness that was in our feet. Back we came on every step we had taken.'

'Story-telling,' said Aunya, 'is the shortening of a road.'

'My blessing on the mouth that taught me!' said the Son, 'I have tales to last the life-time of a man; tales of scaly dragons and witches of the marshes; tales of deep whirlpools and piasts and spells of enchantment: with these I will shorten the road tomorrow.'

On the morrow the Son of the Gubbaun rose in the whiteness of dawn. He put a linen robe on his body. He crowned himself with a chaplet of arbutus that had fruit and blossom. Barefooted he went three times round the Sacred Well, as the sun travels, stepping from East to West. Then he knelt and touched the waters with his forehead and the palms of his hands. He said:

> 'Well of the Sacred Hazels
> Heart of the Hidden Waters
> Well of Wisdom
> Be a deep coolness in my mind,
> Be hidden strength, O Well, in the hour of adversity,
> Show me the truth in the hour of deceit.
> Nourisher of the Rocks
> Life of Waters
> Eye that looks on the Stars
> Let there be love between us.'

Aunya called to him:

'It is time to set out,' she said.

'It is not without advice and without a road-blessing that I am setting out,' said the Son. 'The Well will give me a road-blessing. Give me an advice.'

'Whoever you affront where you are going,' said Aunya, 'put no affront on a woman: for women are the unlockers of secrets, and a woman's hate hunts like the wolf. This is my counsel and I add a gift to it.'

She gave him a rod of the hazel.

'It is likely,' she said, 'that this rod will help you!'

She turned to the Gubbaun.

'It is likely,' she said, 'that you have such a rod yourself.'

'It is more than likely,' said the Gubbaun.

They started.

The distance they had gone was not great when the Gubbaun said:

'Son, shorten the road for me.'

'Story-telling,' said the Son, 'is the shortening of a road!'

'*The oak-wood in the Gap of the Dragon had the redness of Spring on its branches. Midyir's queen came from the Sidhe-Mound, lamenting—*'

'Is the tale sorrowful?' asked the Gubbaun.

'It is sorrowful in parts, but the joyful parts are stronger than the sorrowful parts: and the end is joyful.'

'Continue with it,' said the Gubbaun.

The Son continued. He continued till they came to the Black Waters.

*　　*　　*

At the edge of the Black Waters two of Balor's lords awaited the Gubbaun and his Son. They were cloaked and hooded and closely masked, yet it seemed to the Son of the Gubbaun that under the hood of one of them there was only half a face, and under the hood of the other the head of some strange animal.

'Salutation,' said the half-faced one, and as he spoke the sea of black waters reared itself in waves. 'Salutation to the Wonder-Smith and his son. I am Hrut of the many shapes, the son of Sruth, the son of Sru, the son of Nar, chief and man of might in the country of Balor—and lo, Balor's boat awaits us!'

Huddling against a stairway that Cyclops might have hewn, a boat lay blackly on the Black Waters. It had neither steersman nor galley-slave, neither sail nor oar. Unmoored it swung blankly like a drowned body cast up by the sea.

Without a word the Gubbaun stepped aboard. The Son followed. The hooded lords took their places. Hrut leaned over the stern. He lifted three handfuls of water and flung them against the sky. He gave a loud, piercing, horrible cry.

At that a sea-demon put his shoulder to the boat. He lifted the sea in a curved black foam-smoking precipice in front of the prow—he left it a gaping hollow behind! Short was their crossing.

Harsh was their welcome in Balor's country. A hard bleak desolate wilderness Balor's country was. The sun never lifted his forehead on it. The moon never showed herself. Every blade of grass in Balor's country was like a knife with a drop of venom on the point of it. The jagged stones were scimitar-edged.

'Will it please you, Wonder-Smith, to walk or ride?' asked Hrut.

'To ride,' said the Gubbaun.

Hrut gave a keen piercing cry.

Down THEY swooped out of the air; horribly toothed and clawed, with wings that made a storm about them. Fire came from their nostrils. They bit and clawed one another.

'Will you ride, Wonder-Smith?' asked Hrut.

'I will ride,' said the Gubbaun, 'put bridles on them.'

They put bridles on the biggest one for the Gubbaun, and on the second biggest one for the Son.

'Have you rods,' said the Gubbaun, 'to encourage them, or to chastise them?'

'They encourage themselves,' said Hrut, 'No rider has chastised them. Hold fast. As for us we will trust to our feet.'

The Gubbaun took a master-grip. The son copied him. They rose in the air.

'Oh!' cried the Son, 'it is nothing I have under me but a slanting icy wind, and that is thinning and spreading away—I am falling!'

'Give your fine steed the rod,' said the Gubbaun, 'the Hazel rod!'

The Son of the Gubbaun Saor drew a blow on the wind, and with that the scaly-writhing, fire-breathing, feathered monster took shape under him again. It was so till they struck the fastness of Balor.

Balor's devastating eye was close shut. Hugely the eye-lid weighed upon it, fleshy and sullen. Runes and spells and charms and incantations were on that lid to keep it shut. Balor's face was a blankness. His voice whipped the ears like sleet.

'Build me a dun,' he said, 'strong as the foundations of the earth; a dun with courts and passages and secret chambers; with carvings on the walls of it and carved monsters in the crevices of it; a dun that climbs and blossoms in spires and twists and flame-like billowing curves and fantasies; such a dun as never from the beginning of days shaped itself on the ridge of the world. Gold ye shall have in plenty, and rich jewels and cloaks of honour. Ye shall stagger under the load of your riches. I, Balor, have said it.'

'Such a dun,' said the Gubbaun, 'I can rear.'

The Gubbaun and his Son set to work. They had djinns, and dwarfs, and giants, and goat-footed men, and demons of the air, and fabulous animals, and monstrous beings, and strange beasts to help them. The dun took shape, it grew. There was great delight on the Son of the Gubbaun. He wished with all his heart for a reed flute, but Balor's country was bare of reeds. At length he fashioned a flute of metal, and as he played on it in an idle hour a woman of the Fomor drew close to him. She was poor. She had known hardship. Wrapped in her mantle she held a young child. It was a little while before she spoke. She said:

'For my little son I pray your good will with the music you make. There is a wasting sickness on him and he has no delight in life.'

'I will make a music of delight for him,' said the Gubbaun's Son.

The child put his mother's cloak away from him and peered out. His face was dusky; he had prick ears like a faun; his hair was a black tangled bush standing up on his head; his eyes were golden-yellow and very bright like the eyes a goat has. His eyes pleased the Son of the Gubbaun Saor.

'I will play strength and joy,' he said.

Every day after that the Son of the Gubbaun made music for the Fomor woman and her child. He played away the sickness. He played till the child laughed and danced and tumbled over himself with delight. One day the woman was troubled.

'You have given life and delight to my child,' she said. 'Today he can repay you. My son has one gift from his birth—he can hear the stir of a bird's wing at the other end of the world! No walls can shut a whisper from him: and he has heard a whisper about you. Balor will put you and your father to death when ye have made an end of building the dun, lest a dun the like of it be reared for another. Take counsel therefore with what wisdom is in you and go unharmed from this country.'

The Son of the Gubbaun took that news to his father.

'I must think,' said the Gubbaun, and he sat down.

The djinns sat down. The goat-footed ones sat down. The fabulous animals stretched themselves and licked their paws. There was a marvellous, munificent, soul-gratifying cessation of labour.

Balor's voice split the stillness.

'Let the Gubbaun come before me,' he cried.

The Gubbaun came.

'The work has stopped;' roared Balor. 'Wherefore?'

'The work has stopped,' said the Gubbaun, 'because I am short of a tool that is lying under seven locks in my treasure-chest at home.'

'Give the tokens and signs of that tool,' said Balor, 'my swiftest messenger shall speed for it!'

'I trust no hand but my own on the tools of my trade.'

'Trust your own hand: my messenger shall bring the treasure-chest.'

'The chest is bedded with the foundations of the house: it cannot be moved!'

'If the house holds to the chest,' said Balor, 'my messenger will haul it hither as a net hauls the dog-fish with the salmon.'

He called to one of his most powerful djinns.

'Go,' he said, 'and bring the treasure-chest of the Wonder-Smith hither, though you should bring the ribs of the earth with it!'

'Live for ever, Magnificence,' said the djinn, and was gone.

'He will not come back,' said the Gubbaun Saor.

Balor writhed his lips in a scornful smile.

* * *

Cloaked in gold and vermilion, the sun was stepping into the western sea. The fragrant, amber-coloured air had stillness that was more than music. Aunya stood by the door of the Gubbaun's house. There was stillness and beauty in her face. She watched the sunset. Close to the threshold-stone a furry caterpillar clambered, picking his steps with solemnity and precision. He was a hairy-oubit to delight the heart; his skin like powdered velvet, his hair-tufts carmined and dusted with silver. His head, like an ebon mirror, gave back the sun light. Suddenly a murk of blackness caught the sky, a myriad-plumed gigantic world-engulphing blackness; a rushing, roaring, multitudinous tumult that whirled and spun upon itself; a pre-Cimmerian Cyclopian Centaurian blackness that neared in leaps and bounds and contortions and cataclysms.

Quick as thought Aunya put a shape of magic power on herself. She made herself a spear-point of light against that blackness. The blackness split on it and passed on either side of the house.'

'Messenger of Balor,' said Aunya, 'you have overshot the goal!'

The djinn was angered. He turned: he made himself a raging fire, a tongue of flame against Aunya. He writhed and licked devouringly.

Aunya raised herself in a thunderous-sounding, green, over-toppling wave of the sea.

Hiss-s-s-rt!!! The fire was quenched.

The djinn shook himself clear. He rose up, an icy scimitar-edged relentless-smiting wind of the desert. He smote the smoking sea-wave, he ripped it to shreds of foam: he flung himself flat-edged upon it: he leaned his weight in the thrust of an avalanche: his strokes were hammer-blows, his strokes were lightning-flashes. He howled outrageously, he tied himself into knots. Aunya made herself a drop of water and slid into the earth. The djinn collected himself and drew breath a moment—the wave had gone, no wetness of it glittered!

'Victory,' shouted the djinn. 'A great and utter destruction! I have been too strong.'

Laughter set his ears on edge. Aunya had taken her own shape again and was standing just out of hand-grip.

The djinn made himself an enormous, death-dealing, sickle-clawed, sabre-toothed, tigerish atrocity, and sprang for her! As he leaped, Aunya became a hawk crested with red gold and feathered with white silver. She hung motionless out of reach. She fluttered about his head, moth-like: moth-like she slid between his frantic paws: her talons gripped his shoulder: she buffetted him: she tweaked his tail: she pinched his ears: she tickled his nose: she was on both sides of him: she was above him, and below him, and beyond him, all at once. She was everywhere and nowhere.

At last the great beast rolled exhausted, with the foam of fruitless endeavour clogging and bitter in his mouth.

'Victory leans towards me,' said Aunya.

'Nay,' said the djinn, 'we are too evenly matched to contend thus. We waste time. Let us show each to the other in rivalry what power we are masters of. My power will out-bid yours.'

'So be it,' said Aunya; *'Wit is nimble-footed!'*

'Cunning is more deep-rooted,' said the djinn.

'More to a thick skull suited,' said Aunya.

'Strength gives to wit the lie,' said the djinn.

'Only while strength is by,' said Aunya.

'Strength's claws are sharp and crooked,' said the djinn.

'But wit has wings to fly,' said Aunya.

'Let's leave this rhyming,' said the djinn. 'It is fit only for women. Show me a wonder-feat.'

'I think,' said Aunya, 'that tree-splitting would delight you.'

'It would,' said the djinn.

Close to them was a giant yew-tree. It was older than the oldest ancestor of the eagle: old as the roots of the earth. A tough-knit, mighty-girthed, many-twisted trunk that tree had. Aunya struck it lightly with her hand. The yew-tree split from top to bottom: the redness at its heart was like the redness in a cleft pomegranate.

'Make the tree whole, O djinn,' said Aunya.

'I am a Force of Destruction and Ravage,' said the djinn; 'make it whole yourself'!

Aunya put her hand on the wound—the tree was whole as before.

'Split the tree,' said Aunya.

The djinn bent himself to the work. He made himself a flash of lightning—and slid through the leaves of the tree! He made himself a devastating whirlwind—and drew a singing note from the tree! He made himself a toothed weapon—he blunted, he shivered himself—and there was not a scratch on the tree!

'Does it out-task you, Son of Destruction?' asked Aunya.

'I could split a small branch,' said the djinn, 'if I tried!'

'You have not enough strength,' said Aunya, 'to hold two branches apart if you perched in a fork of the tree to get your breath again!'

The djinn made a leap for the tree and sat himself in a fork of it.

'Close! branches,' said Aunya.

They closed, and nipped the djinn: tighter and tighter they nipped him.

'My grief and my destruction,' cried the djinn: 'I am lost. Take victory, Aunya, and let me out.'

'I will give you room to sit at your ease,' said Aunya, 'but no more. Sit there till the Gubbaun Saor and his Son come home. When their feet cross the house-threshold I will give you freedom: and more than that, the length of your ears in two gold earrings for luck.'

'A swift home-coming to the Gubbaun Saor and his Son!' said the djinn:

> *May the earth hasten their footsteps,*
> *May water smooth the paths for them,*
> *May the wind hustle them forward.'*

'My own wish,' said Aunya: 'Sit there: you will see the sunrise: you will see the young crescent moon: you will see the greenness of grass.'

She left him.

'I'll put ears on me a mile long,' said the djinn to himself as he braced his shoulders in the fork of the bough, and took deliberately and with care the position of greatest ease.

*   *   *

Balor's country awaited the return of the djinn. The hours and days went by. A fury of expectancy wasted Balor. The Gubbaun Saor was calm.

"Twould be well for myself and my son to lose no more time,' said he; 'it would be well for us to set out now, for the bringing back of the tool.'

'My dignity would be lessened,' said Balor, 'if the compulsion of that errand were on you. I will send an embassy: like a conquering potentate, like a royal personage, that Tool shall enter my dominions!'

'To your son alone,' said the Gubbaun Saor, 'will I give the tokens of my wonder-tool: with him shall go the chief Vizier of your kingdom.'

'So be it,' said Balor; 'I will send my son: Powers and Principalities shall accompany him.'

The Gubbaun Saor gave the master-word to Balor's son.'

'The name of the tool is:

Cam 1.n-aġaıó an caım, cor 1 n-aġaıó an cuır, aġus cor 1 n-aġaıó ġanġaıɒe.'

Balor's son said it over, nine times, to himself. He was satisfied then that he had it. He called for his robes of embassy, he marshalled the Powers and Principalities: he arranged their ranks for the White Unicorns and the Kyelins with tufted ears: he saw that the Green Dragons and the Scarlet and Purple Chimaeras were linked with chains of silver. Boastful were his words to the Fomorian Lords: 'Candles of Valour,' he said, 'do not grudge your transcendency to a country ignorant of Balor. Ye shall cast lustre upon it.'

With an earth-shaking sound of trumpets that ranked magnificence set forth.

Day rounded day till its return. Its return was an amazement. A sound of ullagoning went before it.

'Wye-hoo! Wye-hoo! Wye-hoo!
Bal-a-loo! Bal-a-loo!
Ai! Ai! Ai!
Ul-a-loo! Ul-a-loo!
Ul-a-loo!
Kye-u-belick!'

39

Wayside folk, hearing that lamentation, hastened to prostrate themselves and to cover their faces lest they might see how great lords of the Fomor beat their breasts and tore their hair, casting dust on their foreheads. Like a slow wounded snake the procession dragged itself onward.

> *'Wye-hoo! Wye-hoo! Wye-hoo!*
> *Bal-a-loo! Bal-a-loo!'*

That lamentation filled the courts of Balor. Laggard footsteps followed it. Balor's hand groped spearwards. He could not see the grief-dishevelled lords or the anguished abandonment of their prostrations. He dared not open that solitary terrible eye!

'Speak!' he thundered.

The Most Distinguished Personage in that distinguished train raised a dust-grimed head.

'O Balor, O Lord of Life,' he began, 'have pity on us! Misfortune has overwhelmed us: grief eats and gnaws upon us. Your Son, the Light of our Countenances, is in captivity: and the great Vizier likewise. Say the word, O Magnificence, that will rescue them from strait and bitter bondage, and from the terrible country of Ireland—a country where the mind is bewildered: a country where the eyes find no rest: for the earth is a glittering emerald and the sky a blinding sapphire, the sun is a scorching fire and the moon a blistering whiteness. A country where there is no solace for the heart'!

'Cease your lamentations,' said Balor,' 'and tell what has befallen.'

'We came,' O Dispenser of Fate, 'to the house of the Gubbaun. The woman of the house received us. The most illustrious and splendid Prince, your Son, recited to her the tokens of the Tool:

> Cam i n-aȝaiṫ an Caim,
> Cor i n-aȝaiṫ an Cuir,
> aȝus
> Cor i n-aȝaiṫ an ȝanȝaiṫe.

'True is the token,' said the woman of the house; 'I will unbar the treasury for you and the seven locks of the treasure-chest. Enter, Son of Balor; enter, Vizier of Balor.'

They entered, but they came not forth. The woman came forth. 'Go hence,' she said, 'and tell your king that in the treasure-chest of the Gubbaun his son is shut—a grip that will not loosen! With him is the Vizier, fastened down with seven locks. There they will measure time by the heart-beat and the shadow and fraction of a heart-beat till the Gubbaun Saor and his Son cross the threshold-stone of this house: whole and sound as they set out from it.'

'O Balor, O Mountain of Munificence, say the word. Let the Gubbaun Saor and his Son go for their Tool!'

The Most Distinguished Personage prostrated himself afresh.

'*Wye-hoo! Wye-hoo! Wye-hoo!*' sobbed the Unicorns and Chimaeras.

'Balor,' said the Gubbaun, 'the lid of my treasure-chest is heavy, the sides of it are straight and narrow. Let me and my son go for the tool.'

Balor made a frantic gesture with his hands. 'Go!' he cried.

Lords of the Fomor ushered forth the Gubbaun and his Son. Carefully they ushered them, like folk who guard a treasure, yet with an urgency of speed. Soon they stood on the terraced height of Balor's fortress. A sky pale as an ice-field was above their heads: a thousand fathoms below, a river pooled itself blackly. About them towered a wilderness of mountain-peaks; peaks, one-footed, craning upward, blind and insatiable; peaks like contorted monsters, inscrutable; peaks like a gigantic menace, dizzied to the fantasy of a nightmare—arid and hostile.

'Bring steeds for us'! said the Gubbaun.

Hrut, the son of Sruth, the son of Sru, the son of Nar, stepped forward. He flung his voice into the air in a shrill ringing cry—like colour spilt on ice it shivered on those monstrous pinnacles. The sky blackened. The air swirled and eddied to an impact.

Biting, clawing, tangled together, THEY descended.

'Bridle them!' said the Gubbaun.

Lords of the Fomor put bridles on them.

'Health and Prosperity be with you'! said the Gubbaun, his hand on a bridled neck.

'Health and Prosperity!' said the Son.

THEY rose, shaking storm from their wings, cavorting and hurtling, plunging and rearing through the steeps of air.

'Snails!' cried the Gubbaun, 'have ye no swiftness?'

It was thus that the Gubbaun Soar and his Son returned to Ireland.

*   *   *

When the Gubbaun Saor and his Son set foot again in Ireland the earth was glad at their coming: a Wave in the North reared itself and fell with a sound of clangorous bells and loud-voiced trumpets: a Wave in the East reared itself and fell with a sound of clashing cymbals and shrill-voiced flutes: a Wave in the South reared itself and fell with a sound of sweet singing voices, mingling with and over-mastering the sound of timpaun and cruit and bell-branch: and all along the islands of the West and the rocky inlets went a singing reedy whisper *'Mananaun! Mananaun'!*

The rhythm of that welcoming music was a pulse of joy in the flowering grasses: the strong oaks knew it: the white bulls of the forest moved to it, tossing their moon-curved horns: it set the sea-hawks sliding down the wind, stooping in circles: it was a hand-clapping and a shout of laughter in the mountain torrents.

'A noble land and good is Ireland,' said the Gubbaun, 'my thousand blessings on it!'

Aunya made a great Feast of Welcome for them. From the four corners of the world folk came to that Feast: some that had praise-mouthed names and a proud lineage, and some that had a virtue in them of such a strange and subtle essence that it escaped a clamorous recognition. Harpers came, and sweet-voiced women, and men of learning. Kings' sons came to it riding upon white stallions with their manes and tails dyed purple, bells and apples of gold on their bridle reins: the workers in brass and copper the proud makers of beautiful things came to it, and simple poor folk came with good-will in their hearts. The Chief-Poet of Ireland came, with thirty princes in his train, a slender dark-visaged man, his hair wound upon and bound with twists of gold, his singing-robe on his shoulders that only the Chief-Poet might wear: curiously wrought it was of the feathers of bright-coloured birds. There was a king from the North, blue-eyed and huge of limb, he that was lord of dragon-prowed ships: there was a queen from the South, a woman that had many lovers. She had a pale radiant face and eyes the colour of the sky when twilight purples it—she was everywhere the one Rose of Delight. And from the Faery Hills there came three Cup-Bearers so beautiful it was a heart-ache to look upon them for they had unwithering youth beautiful as light dancing on the sea-waves—beautiful as the apple-bough beyond our reach!

The Sheeoga came, the Little People, the Small Folk of the Mountains, they who put mortals astray, for a jest, covering the pathways: or crowd upon them like comrades, running before and behind, and on either side, most joyous of helpers, to show the gaps and pick safe footing through the quagmires—mindful of freshly-querned meal set in beechen bowls for them and porringers of sweet milk. They came in their multitudes and their multitudes, they joined hands and danced round the house, laughing. Aunya sent them out a silver cup brimmed with mead: as quickly as it was emptied it filled again. They never gave it back and it is likely that even to this day it is stravaguing the world in their company.

Within the Gubbaun's house the candles of a king's feast were lighted. The djinn was there—he had measured the length of his ears by the height of the door-lintel. The Great Vizier was there, uncobwebbed of the treasure-chest. Balor's Son was there, splendid in his robes of embassy. The Hound Failinis was there, and a Phoenix-Bird that came out of Tir-nan-oge.

The feast began: it went from lavishness to lavishness, it was jewelled with strangeness as a daggerhilt is crusted with gems. Towards the close the Gubbaun raised a great Cup of crystal in his hands. The wine in it shone like a ruby: it was wine from Moy-Mell.

'Drink!' he cried, 'Let each one drink to the measure of his thirst: the Cup is a well of plenty, it renews itself.'

The Cup went from guest to guest, and each one that held that Marvel in his hands drank to the thing he desired to honour. When the Cup came to Balor's Son he rose up and said:

'*To Balor the Munificent, and to the noble dun that is a-building!*'

The Cup flew into a thousand splinters. The wine ran down like blood.

'Dragon of Death!' cried Balor's Son, 'what evil omen is this?'

'The venom of untruth has shattered the Cup,' said the Gubbaun, 'Balor's munificence was treachery. But not for this thing shall the Cup be destroyed.' He gathered the fragments in his hand. 'Let truth make it whole:

'*Balor plotted my death and the death of my Son when the dun was finished.*'

The Cup became whole in the Gubbaun's hand.

'But,' said Balor's Son, 'in the presence of the lords and chiefs of the Fomor you named the Tool: you gave the Master-Word.'

'I named my Tool,' said the Gubbaun.

> 'The Crooked—against crookedness.
> The Twist—against a twist:
>   and
> The Twist—against treachery:

That tool I needed: that tool my hands can handle now. *I drink to the time when Balor will know that gods are not jealous of godhead!*'

The Gubbaun drank till not a drop remained in the Cup.

'Tell Balor,' he said, 'that the envious heart drips poison on its own wounds, but munificence begets munificence. His mind imagined a palace: let him build it—he has the multitudinous centuries for leisure! But this one night is ours for joy and song. Let music sound, and let the jugglers now toss up the glittering balls.'

Tulkinna the Peerless One stepped forward. He had nine golden apples and nine feathers of white silver and nine discs of findrui-ney. He tossed them up. They leaped like a plume of sea-spray: they shone like wind-stirred flame: they whirled like leaves rising and falling. He wove them into patterns. He made them whirl like motes of dust. They danced like gauze-winged flies on a summer's eve. They tangled the mind in a web of light and darkness till at last it seemed that Tulkinna was tossing the stars.

Then came a burst of light-hearted music.

The djinn danced with the Phoenix-bird.

Aunya danced with Balor's Son.

The Chief Vizier danced with a woman out of Tir-nan-oge.

The Gubbaun Saor's Son danced with the queen from the South.

The sun and moon the stars and constellations danced to the measure of that dancing. The memory of it was honey in the mind of poets for a thousand years: it was riotous heady mead, it was wine in the veins of warriors for a thousand years, and to this hour it is laughter in the heart of the hills.

THE DEATH OF MACHA GOLD-HAIR

Dermot O'Byrne

The harper Airbreach sat at Queen Macha's feet. He loved her and had been loved by her, but during this night of the great Beltaine feast his spirit was heavy within him. Occasionally he writhed impatiently on the low dragon-carved stool upon which he sat, and glanced up angrily and passionately into the lovely and mask-like face of the queen. Yet never once had she even looked at him. Perfectly motionless she sat on the great high-seat, whose cunning and beautiful fashioning was almost entirely hidden by the quantity of wolf- and deer-skins heaped about it that the fair body of the queen might recline in comfort during the feast.

Following a custom first ordained by herself, the harpers were ranged before the high-seat in the form of a half moon, for Macha liked to be girdled with music at all times. The ancient Muirteach, who crouched on his stool figured with grotesque fish and dragon-shapes immediately before the queen, had composed a rann:

> 'As the foamy swift-footed milk-crested wave of the south
> Calls to the pleasant shores of smooth-sanded Eire
> The desirous sweet-lipped surf of our singing
> Is raining about the star-woman, the queen Macha of gracious
> words.'

This tribute had so greatly pleased the queen, that as a mark of her special favour she had bestowed upon the old bard a magnificent golden torque that was wont to circle her throat, and with her own hands had fastened it still glowing with the warmth of her sweet flesh about the neck of the aged minstrel. All the other bards had become inflamed with jealousy, and not content with criticising with rancour the technical merits of the rann, had made several attempts secretly to poison its author, though as yet without success.

From where Macha was seated she could see with ease every corner of the great dun. Though it was fashioned externally of clay and wattles rudely enough, the interior was, after the fashion of the time, not wanting in beauty and even splendour. New rushes had been strewn upon the floor and the damp walls were overhung with sumptuous skins and even in places with tapestries, many of which were already rotted and mildewed with the sticky ooze of the soaked clay beneath them.

The dun was lit with blazing rushes twisted tightly into a kind of plait, dipped in the fat of animals, and mounted in fantastically carven metal braziers. They burned badly, giving forth a very evil smell, and as they were continually going out with much hissing and sputtering several attendants had been set apart for the sole purpose of trimming and relighting them. The hour was late and the feasting was over long since, but still the flagons of mead passed precariously from hand to hand. Most of the 'ceanns' and nobles and many of the women were drunk and the floor was strewn with the inert bodies of warriors, ollavs, genealogists, amazons and maidens mingled almost indistinguishably, some rolling feebly alone among the soiled rushes, whilst others lay dully folded in one another's embraces, their heavy listless arms tightly interlaced, often as it seemed almost unconsciously.

The captain of the guard lay on his back in the middle of the floor, his glazed eyes staring without expression at the damp and oozing roof, and his right arm vaguely waving above him his drinking-cup, skilfully hammered out of the bleached skull of one of his foes. He mumbled quarrelsomely of his own exploits, whilst the paint and sweat dripped off his face into the rushes of the floor.

But the bards circled about the feet of the queen were sober to a man, not from inclination, but because they knew well that a false chord or a forgotten word meant instant death. All through the night they had sung almost unceasingly, but the queen was in very ill humour, and they were disheartened and ill-at-ease. Airbreach, close to Queen Macha's impatiently-tapping sandalled foot, glanced up again into her staring unfathomable face. The air in the dun was stifling, filled with the heavy odour of human bodies and the fumes of mead and wine.

Airbreach felt very dizzy, and he was not sure what thing might happen in the next moment. He drew a deep breath, and with that inhalation seemed to suck into his being a wandering flame that instantly set light to some primitive fury smouldering in the depths of his spirit. He shuddered slightly, and making a convulsive movement with his whole body leapt to his feet. His face was very pale, yet a red spot burned in the centre of each cheek. Tossing the long black hair out of his eyes, he smote several loud sour chords from his harp, and unheeding the fact that two of the strings had snapped beneath his fierce fingers sang:

'Woe to the sweet-tongued bard
And the hero skilled in combat,
He to be putting faith in the smiles of women,
And the honey talk of a high queen;

His soul to be trapped in the snare of desire,
In foolish and profitless things,
The poisonous net of her hair
And the pale mists of her flesh.

If I saw the hawks of the machair,
The fierce broad-winged eagles of western Sliabh Sneachta,
And I after gazing at the haughty queen,
My heart tormented in the bitter heat of the night,
I would say that those were gentle things.

I cry to the gerfalcons of the Red Gap,
The grey-backed very swift swallows of Dooish of the winds,
That they traverse the six roads of green Fodhla
And circle the winds with their strong flight,
My words scorching their tongues
Till they shower them over the world.

The wounds in my middle cry to you,
O wild birds, and this my message,
Macha, the comely queen
Of the glens of western Uladh,
The white-shouldered woman of Tír Conaill,
Is without gentleness, without honour,
Without warmth, without affection,
Without love of poet's words
And the roaring of the harps,
An empty flagon, a hollow reed,
A blasted birch-tree, a false string,
Blown foam on the shifting sands,

A whirl of dust on the dry roads of the world,
Vain as all vain things,
Vain with the vanity of women.'

Throwing the harp to the floor, Airbreach burst into a roar of
bitter mocking laughter and stood before the queen, his breast
heaving and his body swaying as though he were drunk.

When she had first understood the meaning of the the harper's
song, Macha's face had flushed violently, but now she was very
pale. She bit her lip, and her eyes seemed to search some icy
distance. Then she smiled slightly. There were those in the dun
who trembled seeing that smile.

'Cut out his tongue,' said Macha simply, and she smiled again,
and then sat very still, though her bosom rose and fell like a stormy
sea.

The kernes rushed upon the harper, and after binding him,
seized his long dark hair and wrenched back his head. Then they
battered on his mouth with the butt-end of a short spear until the
teeth were driven in, and one of them drawing forth his sgian
hacked out the tongue.

Macha sighed. 'Bring it to me,' she said. They laid the tongue
on a silver dish and placed it before the queen. She looked at it
curiously for a moment, and then a wave of fury appeared to flood
her whole body. She trembled violently and her cheeks became
more red than the wine-stains upon the rushes of the floor.
Drawing a golden pin from her hair, many times with its delicate
point she stabbed the tongue, about which the blood was already
beginning to congeal. Then she rose to her feet, her chin thrust
out, and her face lime-white even to the lips. She swept over the
floor, the rushes hissing beneath her long scarlet robe, to the edges
of which some of them clung. Laughing low and derisively, she
stood before the harper.

'Airbreach, Airbreach,' she said softly, 'where now will you be
finding any white woman to kiss those lips that a thousand windless
nights among the dewy hills have lied so sweetly that the stars and
the lake-waters have listened to thee even as thy love has listened?
Between what fragrant breasts shall thy mouth that was beloved
of queens whisper its music now in the secret corners of the house
when lights are overturned?'

And she pointed her white forefinger, the nail dyed with a costly red spice, at the battered swollen bleeding thing that had once been the mouth of a great poet.

'Sing to me, Airbreach, my poet of the golden voice,' she went on with false tenderness, 'Sing to me one of thy songs that are more sweet than the music of the nightingales of Coillsheogue, and more heady than the red mead the rivers pour among the flowers of Magh Mell, the pleasant plain. Sing to me "The Waving of the Corn," with which men say the hearts of the proudest women are melted, as the snows of Errigal are melted in a single night by the warm honey-breath of golden-eyed Bel.' The eyes of the harper rolled expressionlessly in his bloodstained and contorted face. Even in his agony the queen seemed to hold him fascinated, as some lovely and evil she-snake fascinates her prey.

'Sing! sing! sing!' cooed Macha, relentlessly, 'I thirst for thy songs as a hero thirsts for battle, as the weary for sleep, as the night for the dawn.' She leaned forward, her eyes close to his staring and strained eyes, and suddenly she stamped her foot in simulated wrath.

'Thou wilt not sing,' she screamed savagely, and her eyes blazed. 'Cowherd! Mule! Clod! Ha, ha, ha! thou hast made very sweet music in thy day upon yonder harp, now shall thy harp make music upon thee!'

She made a sign to the chief of the kernes, pointing at the harp which lay among the tossed and trampled rushes, most of its strings already hanging tattered over the edges of the frame. But before any of them could make a movement an exulting cry rang out and from the listless and stupefied throng a woman leapt with the activity of a wild cat, trampling heedlessly on bare faces and arms in the fury of her wild rush. She was of abnormal height and clad in a single skin garment. Her muscular tanned legs were bare, and her thick black hair hung in matted dishevelled clusters over her eyes. Between her left eye and the corner of her mouth a long livid scar stretched, and the slipping aside of her loosely folded garment revealed the fact that her right breast had been burnt off according to the usual custom of warrior women, a practice which allowed the spear-arm greater freedom of action. Thrusting aside the blear-eyed staggering warriors, she snatched up the heavy clairseach with a sweeping movement of the arm as she ran.

The pain-clouded eyes of the doomed harper regarded her with a kind of dull surprise. For a moment she stood looking through

her tangled hair into those eyes. Then she shook herself like some
wild animal, and with a scream swung the clairseach above her
like a battle-axe. As it fell one of the drunken women lying upon
the floor cried out in terror and began to whimper, but the blows
still continued to rain down. With the heavy embossed frame of
the harp the amazon battered Airbreach's head until the bones of
the skull were crushed and the blood spurted out upon the rushes.
She laughed, feeling the hot dark drops dripping from the harp
upon her hands and bare arms. And she chanted this rann:

> 'Aïa, Aïa, O—ro!
> Long shall the day be remembered
> In the dun of Cliath-na-Righ,
> In the goodly wide-spreading feast-house
> Of Macha of haughty eyebrows.
> Long shall this day be remembered,
> The night of the Bleeding of the Harp,
> The harp of Airbreach Honey-mouth
> Whose singing was a sword-edge,
> A moonlit drift of blossom,
> A wave on the shores of the heart.
> Long shall the day be remembered
> In the grianans of western Tír-Conaill,
> The day when the strings that were wont
> To stream with songs of passion
> Sweated with blood and death.'

When she had finished this chanting she dropped the harp and
fell swooning as it seemed across the dead body of the poet, her
face pressed into his breast.

Macha had regarded the scene with startled eyes that for the
moment under the sway of astonishment appeared almost innocent
and childlike, but the sudden silence which followed the amazon's
chant broke the spell. The queen turned her head away contemptu-
ously with a short laugh that seemed wrung from her throat almost
involuntarily. There was a moment of silence, and then a strange
sadness passed over the queen's face as a cloud floats across the
hard blue midday sky. She stared abstractedly at the aged Muirteach's head, bent in some grievous reflection, his long silver hair
falling forward among the strings of the *cruit* that rested on his

knees. 'The waving of the corn!' she murmured slowly into the depths of her shining hair. She started with a gesture of irritation. 'I am weary,' she said fretfully, 'lead me to the grianan. I will that only women sleep with me tonight. I tire of men and their foolishness.'

The women led her down the length of the dun, the proud feet of the queen stepping delicately as those of a hind among the rushes stained with blood and wine. Her beautiful head, poised with marvellous grace on her white shoulders, was motionless, her eyes stared forward without expression. Already she seemed to have forgotten the tumultuous happenings of the evening. As she moved the little golden balls suspended to the ends of the four twisted plaits in which her yellow hair was dressed swayed languidly and rhythmically upon her graceful back, and the amethyst brooch that fastened the scarlet embroidered robe glittered now and again with unearthly and disturbing hues as the flickering gleam of the rush-lights fell momentarily upon it.

For a long time a profound silence had reigned in the dun. Then there was a very faint rustling somewhere among the rushes followed by a soft swift pattering sound. A rat ran across the skins on the floor and leaping upon the daïs began to gnaw one of the carven legs of the high-seat. Another half-hour passed, and then a pale shaft of moonlight stole through the single small opening that served the great dun as door and window. It moved slowly to the right, revealing for a moment perhaps the flushed face and swollen eyes of some sleeping reveller. It seemed to be searching for something, timidly, tenderly, as some fragile woman searches a star-lit battle-field for the body of her love. It swayed forward slowly and obliquely, every moment becoming more and more narrow, until finally, slender as the shaft of a spear, it fell upon the body of the dead Airbreach, on the blood, stiff, dark, and clotted about the wrecked milk-white face, on the obscure living shape stretched upon that lifeless shape, and the heavy hair spread about the pale breast like a thundercloud. The moonlight seemed to cling to those two for a moment and then stole softly away, leaving the dun in unfathomable darkness.

Towards morning Macha the queen awoke with a start, the grianan was strangely hot and she felt an unusual and painful sensation at her throat, as though wires were being twisted about it and were gradually biting into her flesh. She became furiously angry. With one hand she groped for the knife that was always her bedfellow in the darkness, whilst with the other she clutched her soft neck, but under her trembling fingers she felt nothing but the smooth firm flesh.

She opened her eyes, closed them again in terror, opened them once more. A heavy red glare smote upon them, and something smelling acrid and sour wreathed about her, flooding the glare in dense swelling clouds. Fire and smoke! She tried to scream, but those wires about her throat strangled the sound. She lifted herself upon her elbow with a supreme effort, for her body seemed turned to stone. She attempted to draw a full breath but was unable to do so. Something seemed to be straining and tearing her breasts, strange lights and darknesses swam before her eyes, there was a buzzing sound in her ears as though some bee had strayed into her brain and was striving to escape.

Through the smoke and the glare she could see the forms of her women lying as if in sleep, most of them quite still. Near to her one of them writhed languidly, heaving up her body for a moment and then falling back, as it seemed to the queen with a certain dreadful luxuriousness. She did not move again.

Macha was afraid of death, and the heat was becoming every moment more intense. It seemed that spears were piercing her eyes outward from behind and that they must fall from her head in the next instant. She tried to rise, but some force pinned her down to the bed. With a fearful struggle that seemed to tear the heart from her breast she gained her feet and stood reeling, the red glare wrapping like a lover her beautiful naked body, over which as it seemed to her a thousand envenomed tongues were sliding. She tottered this way and that, hiding her mouth in her hair, and seeking for some door of escape.

Suddenly she heard a sound of singing as it seemed at an immense distance. The queen's brain became confused. At times the singing melted into the flames, at others it seemed the flames sang, and again she thought that in those red-tongued darting things she was actually looking upon the very forms of those bitter passion-wrung sounds. It was indeed a bitter singing that night for Queen Macha Gold-hair.

'Hei-a! Hei-a! Hei-a-aha!
A red night for Cliath-na-Righ,
For the shining grianan of Macha Oir-cinn.
Sweet the song of the flames to the stars,
A music passing that of stately harps,
Masterful the red red lips
Kissing the breasts of the queen,
The tossing burning arms
That are wreathed in her tressy hair,
Hei-a! Hei-a!—Aro! Aree!
The four winds of green-pastured Eire,
The lean hungry winds
Furiously follow the fire,
The brown wind of the west, the moon in his hair,
The red wind of the east, his feet stained with the sun-blood,
The grey wind of the south, the rain in his eyes,
The black wind of the north, the storm froth on his mouth,
Ochone, ochone, aree!
The pale lips of the dawn
Will be crying after Macha the queen,
The blown sands in the dry sea-grasses
Shall answer with voices weak, faint, very thin.
The smooth very gracious body of her
That was as flowers that fall through foam,
The breasts that were apples on a sunny bough,
The hair that was ripe corn in the summer wind,
The mouth that was as the berry of the rowan,
All these are dust, a very little dust,
And it lying between the fingers of the four winds
In the sundered mists of the western world,
That cling to the four great mountains
Of surgy foam-worn Eire.
My grief for him that is the beloved
Of two pitiless fierce-eyed women!
Evil shall come to him from the sun,
And misfortune among the rains of the moon,
Neither shall he find peace in the hollow hills.
Aio, hei-a, aha! O Macha of the scornful brow,
My laughter leaps in the flames,
Sure I am after drowning you in the great fires of my mirth!'

The queen's head fell back, she clutched her breast with both hands. Dimly she heard a great crashing and splitting as the sides of the grianan fell in roaring. Through the glares and blacknesses circling giddily in her eyes she saw indistinctly the figure of a woman that leapt over the breach and was instantly lost in a wilderness of flame.

THE OUTLAW

Joseph O'Neill

*   *   *

Across the street to the right a man was being led out of the King's Borg by his guards. In front of the Borg, between it and the city gate a crowd had collected. As the man passed through it with hands bound behind his back he was a fair mark for them. Yells filled the air. Sticks and stones were flying. The guards drew away from the man leaving a space for the missiles.

'Come along,' Eric cried, dragging Olaf.

He was as excited as the crowd by the common fury against the man, though Olaf was sure he didn't know him. Olaf didn't wonder at this, though he himself felt nothing. Then the man's eyes, glancing round, rested on his. Immediately his feelings changed. He began to yell at him.

'Claim the right to run the gauntlet. You've the right to run the gauntlet—claim it. Claim it.'

The people round Olaf turned and stared at him, but he kept on shouting.

The man heard him, turned on his guards.

'The gauntlet!—the gauntlet! I claim the right to run it.'

'Let him run it—It will be better sport,' yelled a voice.

Then the whole crowd was yelling:

'Let him run it—let him run it.'

'He has to be brought to the doom-ring first. He must run the gauntlet from there,' said the Captain of the guards.

'Let him be brought there,' shouted the crowd.

'But he must be brought there uninjured. He must get his full chances.'

'Right! right!' they yelled.

The guards led the man towards the town-gate and through it. As he walked through the crowds he kept turning his head, looking at the women he was passing, the King's men in their red cloaks who were holding back the crowd, a ship tented-over which was floating out on the river opposite the town.

'He has the look of a man going to a festivity, not the look of a man going to the Doom-ring,' Olaf said to Eric.

'I've seen a lot of them that way as if they were looking forward to the unusual thing they were going to experience,' said Eric who had become calm again.

'Perhaps it's because he's to get a chance for his life.'

'It isn't. I've seen them like that when they had no chance. Those of them that weren't dead of anguish already were often looking forward to it, especially slow men. You'll find he's a slow sort of man, sluggish.'

'It's the resurrection they are looking towards, perhaps,' said Olaf.

'It isn't. I've seen as many heathens die that way as Christians, men who believed in nothing after death.'

'Then it's death itself they're looking forward to.'

'It can't be that. It's something else, an elation about something else. I've heard men confess it afterwards, some who escaped. I can see the same feeling in that fellow's face.'

'If I were going to be broken on the Doom-ring, I believe I would find the faces of the people I passed hard to understand, if they looked like the faces round us,' said Olaf. 'They would become things, not men or women any longer,' he added.

'I never think of death,' said Eric. 'Whenever I got a wound, even a deep one, it healed quickly.'

'You never even thought of dying well.'

'No. I never think of dying at all. Why should I? When they talk about dying like a Viking, I always say to myself "Why talk of things like that?"'

They were coming near the Doom-ring, a wide circular platform on the high ground near the mouth of the Dodder. The man was mounting the steps, looking down at the crowd. Behind the platform and the crowd on the river side, he could see rows of horses' faces. The country people had come to the town to see him being broken in the Doom-ring. There were also two bear-cubs at the Borg that a Norse trader had brought as a present to the King and they wanted to see them. Some of them also hadn't finished hiring their Spring workmen or collecting Winter debts. There were a good many reasons for coming in, and, as the country people had outspanned near the fiord, there was a big crowd on that side, as well as on the town side.

The man was standing on the Doom-ring mound, taking account of all this and drawing deep breaths. The double crowds made his chances less.

The guards freed him, untied his hands, led him to the edge of the Ring.

In front of him women who had been going through the crowd selling boiled eggs and cold fish, stood to stare up at him.

'He must get ten yards' grace,' the Captain said to the crowd.

They drew back, tense, waiting.

'Farther! Farther!' cried the guard. He freed the man.

'Now,' he said to him.

For a few moments the man still looked round at the crowd. Then he bounded towards the river. As he sprang, a roar went up from hundreds of throats. Sticks, stones flew at the flying figure.

He swerved, dodged. The shower of missiles was all round him, but it saved him from closer attack. A heavy stone struck him. He fell, got up again. The crowd was running towards the river to head him off.

'The Chapel! The Chapel beyond the South Wall,' Olaf yelled.

The man swung to the right, away from the river. The crowd swung round, yelling with the joy of the chase, but his change of direction had given him a breathing space.

Then Olaf remembered that there were men barking the oak-trees near the Chapel for his father's tannery.

'They'll cut him off,' he thought, 'drive him back to the crowd.'

He began to run. The man was to the left, running with long loping strides, towards the South City Wall. He had more than his ten yards' grace now, nearer fifty, and he was gaining on his pursuers. But the bark-cutters would get him, strike him down or head him back.

Olaf was in front of the crowd. If he could get to the bark-cutters before they harmed the man, they would be a help, as they were his own men and would take his orders.

He ran on breathlessly. He didn't know why he wanted to save this man. He had often hunted with the crowd when outlaws ran the gauntlet, but today there was some change in his mind, some feeling of comradeship when the man had looked at him.

They had rounded the corner of the city wall. The little chapel was in view, a man in priest's garb standing at the door, the bark-cutters standing in a bunch to the left looking towards them.

The fugitive swerved to the left. The bark-cutters began to run to cut him off.

'Don't cut him off—save him—save him,' Olaf yelled to them.

The men stopped, looking from Olaf to the fugitive.

'He's to be rescued!' Olaf shouted to them. 'Knui! Knui! To the rescue!'

He turned and faced the crowd. The bark-peelers came running up.

'Keep them back! Hold them back!' he cried to them.

The men spread out in a line facing the crowd. As they spread out they drew their knives.

The crowd halted, puzzled by what had happened.

'He's no kin to you or Ulf,' a man shouted to Olaf.

'He's my man!' Olaf cried back to him. 'Besides,' he said, 'He has got to sanctuary.'

He pointed towards the chapel. The man had reached the chapel door and was talking to the priest.

'He's a heathen,' cried a man. 'He has no right to Christian sanctuary.'

'The priest is accepting him,' cried another.

Aidan, the priest, had taken the man by the arm, was bringing him into the chapel.

'He hasn't any right to accept him,' cried a man.

'But he has the right,' shouted another.

Eric came up to Olaf.

'Why do you want to save him?' he asked.

'Because he has earned his life.'

'But they'll get him when he leaves the chapel.'

'They won't. The King can give him his liberty now that he has earned it by running the gauntlet.'

A light came into Eric's eyes.

'That Viking Captain down at the harbour is short of men. He'd take him if the King lets him go,' he said.

'I'll go to the King at once,' he added.

He was excited, as full of eagerness to save the man now as he had been before to hunt with the crowd.

'Stay beside the chapel,' he said. 'I'll be back in a short while.'

He went towards the crowd.

'I'm going to the King to see about it,' he said. 'You must wait for his decision.'

'You're taking a great deal on yourself, Eric Sorkerson,' said a man.

'I'm not taking it on myself. It's a matter only the King can decide,' Eric answered calmly.

'Eric Sorkerson is right,' cried several voices.

It was evident that the greater part of the crowd was in agreement. It began to break up into groups. The women with the hard boiled eggs and the fish had come up. It was midday. If the man hadn't run the gauntlet they'd have been getting near their dinners by now. So the women were welcome with their cold victuals.

There were other distractions in view also. A man had come from the rear with a brown stallion, a group of men round him.

'They're arranging a horse-fight. They won't trouble us for the present, but keep where you are and don't let them come in,' said Olaf to the bark-peelers, and went off to the chapel.

Before he went in he looked back at the crowd. They were in two groups, round horses which they were bringing towards one another.

Olaf walked to the chapel door, looked in. The man was talking to the priest, telling him his story.

He was a curious-looking fellow, but as Olaf watched him he knew why he had intervened to save him. It was the look in the man's eyes, a curiously trustful look in a heavy old-fashioned sort of face. He wondered how he had got to be an outlaw.

'I'm a man used to either field work or sea-work,' the man was saying to the priest. 'Smith-work and carpenter work come handy to me too, if you want them.'

Olaf looked at his clothes. They were old and worn, but the coarse woollen jacket and the linen breeches were carefully darned and the goatskin shoes were patched neatly.

'I won't hide from you that I'm a man with bad luck who brings bad luck on others,' he was saying now.

'I couldn't employ you,' said the priest. 'Besides, you're a heathen, but I'll save your life if I can.'

Olaf turned back to look at the crowd. The horses—a big brown stallion and a grey with a black stripe on his back—were going round one another trying to get a chance of biting. From the chapel the man's voice came in a low murmur telling the priest about his life; how he became an outlaw. Bits of it came to Olaf.

'Beside the shore, men were sitting round a fire built on stones. On the fire a big kettle was hanging. I knew by the smell that they were boiling fish. Out on the river they had a ship and a ten-oared cutter. The cutter lay beside the rudder of the ship, and the oars were in the loops.'

The yells of the crowd drowned his voice. The owner of the brown stallion had joined in the fight, whipping his horse violently. The horse responded by rising on his hind-legs and biting savagely at the striped stallion's shoulder.

At the corner of the wood near the chapel a couple of tethered goats, troubled by the noise, began to pull each other in different directions. From the chapel, the voice became audible again: 'We didn't plunder, as the land was poor, and we thought it better to ask for a winter home there. It was there I met her. The early winter slaughtering and salting was going on, the women going in and out all day, bringing honey and storing it in the shelves, men too with grain and malts—'

He paused, as if to picture the scene. Olaf could hear the priest's voice murmuring encouragement. Then the outlaw's words came clear again.

'Winter is a good herdsman, priest. She brings all creatures home. There was a woman there, a young woman with long hair down both sides of her bosom and the locks turned up under a belt that caught her scarlet kirtle round the middle. Her face was marked where she had fallen into the trench-fire when she was a child. Also she had little property—'

He stopped as if he was listening to the yells of the crowd. The owner of the striped horse had run under the rearing stallion and thrust at the other man with a stick.

The outlaw was continuing his story.

'I married her. Then one day a woman said to her: "You'd be well enough married if your husband had the name of courage." The eyes don't hide it, if a woman begins to think badly of a man. A little street runs in that town from the house we lived in down to the river and, as I was coming up one day, a woman said to another, "Every woman wants a man, not a mid-day ghost." So I knew what was happening to her.'

A group of riders appeared at the city gate, coming towards the chapel. Olaf recognised Eric amongst them. He went into the chapel and called out:

'The King's messengers are coming with the judgement.'

The man turned his face and Olaf saw that in his story he had forgotten why the King's men were coming. He turned back to the priest.

'I went to the mouth of the river. Fishermen came there,' he said, 'and it was a good place for tidings. It was there I learned about him and her.'

The trampling of horses was loud outside, Eric's voice calling out 'He is free. The Viking Captain is short of men and the King has agreed to let him go with him, if he gives a guarantee not to return.'

The man didn't seem to hear him.

'His courage wasn't so good after all, not as good as she thought,' he said to the priest.

'May God in His mercy pardon you, my son,' said the priest, 'And heal your mind,' he added.

Eric put his head in the door.

'The tide is on the ebb. The ship will be going out with the ebb-tide,' he cried.

The man turned.

'The ebb-tide,' he said, 'the ebb.'

He came out of the chapel.

'Let us get him back to the town while they're engaged with the horse-fighting,' said one of the King's men.

The man turned to the priest.

'If I ever can save a mass-priest, I'll save him, when we're plundering, Herra,' he said.

'Go and God be with you and bring you to His fold,' said the priest.

EARTH-BOUND

Dorothy Macardle

*   *   *

'Do you think that people who are not Irish know what home-
sickness is?' Una said. 'It is harder being away from a country that
is in trouble,' Michael O'Clery answered, 'than from a country

that is at peace. It is not home-sickness only—it is that you want to be in the fight.'

He spoke contentedly. It was his last night in Philadelphia; tomorrow he was going home.

Una's pale little face looked sad in the dying fire-light; the coming and going of Irish friends filled her, always, with joy and pain. Even Frank's keen face grew wistful and, for myself, an unbearable pang of *heim-weh* silenced me.

Una spoke again, after a pause.

'Do you know what I miss more than the people, more than the dear places?' she said. 'It is that sense one has every-where in Ireland—in the glens, and in Dublin—the old squares on the north side, and the quays—of the companionship of the dead.'

Frank laughed in brotherly mockery.

'They stay in Ireland, I suppose, sooner than go to Heaven? Or is it doomed to it they are, instead of Hell?'

But Michael said seriously:

'I believe she's right.'

Michael had something to tell us: that could be felt. It was past midnight but Una put coal on the fire.

Three weeks ago Michael had arrived, without a passport, in Philadelphia, on some mission not to be disclosed, and, like most friendly travellers from Ireland had found his way soon to the young editors of the *Tri-Colour*, Una and Frank O'Carroll. Within their hospitable studio his few idle hours were spent.

Nowhere outside Dublin have I known so shabby yet lovable a room. It was perhaps their one treasure, Hugo Blake's glorious 'Dawn,' that made one seem to breathe there the air of home. That picture is magical. There is nothing painted but the hills of Clare-Galway seen from the water and daybreak in the sky behind, yet it is the dawn of all that Ireland has been waiting for these seven hundred years.

'You could go away from that picture,' Michael said once, 'and die.'

There was little else—brown walls, three uncurtained windows looking down on the square, at evening all blue shadow and amber lights; faded draperies on the divans and many-coloured cushions around the fire; it was enough, with Frank's iridescent, satirical humour and Una's pleasure in her friends, to create an illusion inexpressibly restful. It was the exiles' oasis of living waters at the end of each arid week.

It was late at night, as now, when all but a guest or two had gone, that the talk would grow full of reminiscences and omens and prophesies and dreams, and strange adventures would be told.

Not one word had Michael said, yet, of the perils that followed his escape, but Una's remark had started some deep train of thought in him. He repeated, in a tone of deep conviction:

'I believe she's right.'

'You think they stay—?' I asked.

'Some,' he replied. 'Some that died for Ireland, thinking more of Ireland than Heaven at the end.'

'And they're wanted,' he added gravely. 'They are surely wanted still.'

'Do you know Glenmalure?' he asked then.

I knew it, a deep valley of the Wicklow hills, shut out from life, compelling mournful thoughts.

'They might well be there,' I said.

'I'll tell you a thing happened there,' Michael went on, 'and you can explain it the way you please. It's there Donal and I were on our keeping after we escaped from Mountjoy.'

'Donal O'Donel?' asked Frank.

'Yes; he got a life-sentence, you know, and we were to be transferred to Pentonville. My own sentence was only two years, but I was fairly desperate for him. If you ever knew him you'd understand; he'd never been in a city a week together—a long-limbed mountainy lad, the quickest brain I ever met, extraordinarily confident and proud. He'd a kind of thirst for life for its own sake that you don't find often among the boys, yet the death-sentence seemed to give him a kind of joy; 'twas the commutation he couldn't stand—things looked fairly hopeless, you know, then—and Pentonville for life.

'We knew 'twould be a desperate chance; he had a damaged foot, he'd be hard to disguise too, with his fiery hair; but 'twas worth any risk and we had Pierce O'Donovan outside—the gaol was never built Pierce couldn't break; we made a plan you'd think crazy and got away.

'I'll not forget that night—the sky over us and a grand wind full of rain and a cruel moon and we driving like fury in an open car, clean through the city and over the hills! Half a dozen times we were halted, but Pierce had licences and all and we got through. He put us with an old couple in the last cottage in the glen—Glenmalure—who welcomed us like their own. We were to stay there till Donal's foot would be well, then we'd be sent for to join the column in the hills.

"Twas a strange land to us both—different altogether from Sligo or Donal's place, Donegal: a steep narrow valley in a wilderness of naked hills, all rocks, bracken and dead gorse, treacherous with spots of bog; the hills are channelled everywhere with torrents—you hear the noise of them night and day. Old Moran was forever warning us: "Many a one got lost here and was never found; the Glen doesn't like strangers," he used to say.

'I had no love for the Glen; 'twould be beautiful on the frosty mornings when Lugnacullia had a crest of snow, but in the afternoons—'twas December—when the sun fell behind Clohernagh and the whole place went chill and dark under a vast shadow, you felt drowned . . . I said to Donal it was too like Synge's play. Donal didn't know Synge's play; he never had much use for books; he'd rather be making history than reading it; he loved the Glen: "'Tis a grand place," he said, "heroic; it remembers the old times."

'His foot was better; he could hobble a good way with a stick and we explored the nearer hills on those bright cold mornings—Slieve Moan and Fananieran and Cullentragh. Donal was wild to climb to the Three Lochs, but old Moran made a scare: "There are bog holes you'd sink in and never rise," he said; "'twould be a good man would do it on a summer day, let alone in the snow"; and not a soul in the valley would guide us, so we gave it up.

'One day, though, we followed the torrent to Art's Loch; it was the longest climb Donal had done and he was pleased; a place like that exhilerated him. The sun was setting and there was a red stormy light on the water lying lost there in its hollow among the great hills. Dead solitary the loch is; I thought there was no life in it at all, but Donal was excited: "'Tis these places are haunted," he said, "by the old Chieftains and Kings." He looked like one of them himself standing there with the ruddy light on his face; predestined to victory he looked. A song Mrs Moran used to be quoting came into my head, about "The King of Ireland's son" and "the crown of his red-gold hair," but the sun sank and the shadow rose over him and a black thought crossed my mind—

"He is the sort England always kills." That place would make you afraid of death.

'There was trouble in the glens, we heard; it would likely be after Christmas before anyone would come for us; being ignorant of the country it would be useless setting off by ourselves. We got impatient waiting; maybe we went too freely about the hills; Donal was very heedless with strangers; they'd often stare at him as if wanting to remember his face. Anyway, on Christmas Eve the waiting came to an end.

"Twas a savagely cold day with a wind out of the north and a black sky and folks were staying at home. We sat all the evening with the Morans round a gorgeous fire talking, or rather listening to Donal's talk. He was in one of his keen, inventive moods when he'd plan laws and constitutions and lay out the whole government of Ireland the way you'd tell faery tales to a child. Some of his ideas would startle you, but he'd not let you off till you saw they were sound. He drew a map of Ireland on the bellows with a burnt stick and started planning a military defence; it was a great plan surely that he made. "We could face the nations of the world," he said, "if we had no traitors in our own. Ireland's a natural fortress, the best God made."

'"God keep you!" said Mrs Moran fervently: "God spare you, son!"

'There was a sharp knock at the door and we stood up; old Moran opened; it was a girl, a neighbour's girl, who worked at the hotel; she was wet and breathless and shivering with cold. The Black and Tans were drinking at the hotel; they had raided Glendaloch and Laragh; they were raiding Glenmalure, "For the two lads escaped out of Mountjoy." She had guessed suddenly and deserted her work to warn us—run all the way. "Beasts and devils they are! My God! if you heard the threats and curses! Into the hills with you," she pleaded, "for God's sake!"

'Donal looked at old Moran, "Where will we go?" The old man shook his head wretchedly: "If I could tell you that—" "If you could get to Reilly's at the Three Lochs," the girl said, "they'll not look as far as that; or O'Toole's of Granabeg, or Mr Barton's; but you'll not get so far; you'd have to pass Glendaloch."

'Mrs Moran was parcelling up food and sobbing, "My God! My God! the boggy hills and the snow, and he with a broken foot!" Snow was falling, steady and deliberate, out of the leaden sky;

Donal looked at it and smiled, the way you'd smile at an enemy; it was better than Pentonville. We thanked brave little Nannie and hugged poor old Mrs Moran and set out, facing north.

'There was the ford to cross, then the precipitous face of Lugduff Mountain to scale; by the time we had clambered to the ridge and looked down on Glenmalure again it was night. We saw through the snowfall white lights rushing along the road below, and shots sounding like volleys echoed among the hills.

'Our way lay over a rugged moorland, unbroken save for boulders and thwarted trees, a waste of bog and heather, stiff grasses and withered bracken all buried in snow; no light or outline of a house was visible; only the curves of the hilltops against the sky. We knew nothing of these regions; nothing of the direction in which any habitation lay; we could only push straight onward and trust to luck, keeping our faces to the wind.

'But there was no luck with us; the snow never ceased falling; not one star shone; each step was a separate labour; the snow drove in our faces; I grew heavy and numb with cold; Donal dragged forward steadily with the help of his stick, but he did not speak at all; I saw his face by the pale gleam of the snow; it was white and grim with pain. He refused angrily to take my arm.

'It comes back like a nightmare now: the two of us plodding on towards nothing, labouring up hill and down again, hour after painful hour, the desert around us looking forever the same; we might have been working in a circle for all I knew. At last Donal reeled and clutched my arm, then stood up, breathing through his teeth. I asked if his foot had given out. "If I could rest it a minute," he gasped; "it's only the lumpy ground . . ."

The snow had lightened a little and we could see: a black heaven and a white earth; sharp granite edges thrusting up through the snow; down hill, to our left, a clump of trees.

'My own feet were like lead, frozen: I was stupefied with cold and could think of nothing to do; I felt a monstrous weight was against us, compassing our destruction: the hills were malignant to us, and the wind, and God. Donal had his senses still; he whispered, "Make for the trees!"

'We reached the clump of firs at last and got a respite from the wind; Donal sank down on a fallen trunk, easing the tortured foot; I leaned against a tree, dizzy; I was afraid to sit down. Already that craving was over me that comes so fatally in snow, to abandon the forlorn, dreamlike struggle and lie down in the soft fleeciness and sleep. But Donal had risen, suddenly, as though called: "Come on," he said tensely, "we mustn't rest."

'We stood together in the open again, wondering which way to go; one way seemed as meaningless as another; all led to the same end. Donal looked at me for a moment remorsefully: "I'm sorry, Mike," he said, "you could have managed it alone."

'I was answering angrily, but he stopped me with "Hush! Look there!" pointing straight in front of him; then he started forward again whispering, "Come on!"

'He was following something; I followed him and at last, through the veil of blowing snow, I saw it too—a tall, dark, striding form.

'A crazy zig-zag course we made, following that far-off figure which never noticed us, never beckoned us, never turned.

'Down a steep rough hillside we went and far along the bank of a frozen stream; up a wooded slope and out once more on a white plain. Dizzied with swirling snow, choked and aching with the cold, we followed—no thought or will left to us of our own.

'Donal stopped short now and then for a moment, paralysed by pain, but limped on again; our guide never stopped; we never came near enough to call to him, never near enough to see more than the lithe, tall figure of a boy moving fearlessly through the night.

'We were travelling over a difficult, stony hillside, steering towards a black grove of trees, when Donal lurched sideways and leaned on my shoulder, his eyes closed. I saw he was done, exhausted, and I held him, looking for our guide. He had gone; he seemed to have disappeared into the trees. But below us lay the road: it would be easier going; it must lead to houses: hope— the hope of dear life—rose up in me, and Donal opened his eyes. "Come on," he said faintly, standing up and then, with a twisted smile, "I'll have to lean on you."

'We had not gone ten yards when the air rumbled with a familiar sound and below us from the right, round the turn of the hill they came driving—those lurching, malignant lights. We were in full view from the road, on the bare hill-side, and those were lorries below.

'I saw them crashing along and stopping, saw the rutty road splashed with brilliance from the headlights; saw the men dismounting and heard a hoarse voice shouting orders as they scattered to left and right.

'I looked at Donal. "Run," he commanded, "I'll follow," and at the first step he pitched headlong and lay on the snow.

'On the hillside opposite, the far side of the road, a searchlight from the lorry began to play. To rise, to attempt to drag or carry Donal would have betrayed us both; he was in a dead faint, his face like marble; I lay down, crouched over him in the snow.

'Men out of the lorries came swarming up, searching with flash lamps, cursing brutally as they came. Then the searchlight swung over and began to play along our side of the hill. The broad beam came creeping over the slope: I saw the intense black and white pictures leap out of the darkness one by one—saw every boulder, every bunch of stubble as it swept steadily towards where we lay. The searchers crossed it, reeling—they were drunk; they carried bayonets; they were Black and Tans. I pulled my gun out and held it at Donal's head—I meant to fire when the light touched us—God forgive me! what else was there to do?

'Then, suddenly, I saw our guide again; down from the cover of the trees he came leaping, between us and the path of light. I heard the triumphant yell of the searchers as the beam caught him full—a tall slim figure with lifted arms. He stood an instant, then ran, swift as a deer, clean across the shaft of light, away from us into the dark again; volleys of shots and a wild clamour of yells followed him as he ran. .

'I staggered to my feet, dazed, half-believing I was in a dream; for I had seen him when the light fell on him—the long limbs and the high head and the red wind-blown hair; I would have sworn a hundred oaths that it was Donal, but Donal lay beside me on the snow.

'The shouts and firing followed the flyer and the sweeping light followed him over the hill. The lorries were turned and followed, driven madly along the road, and we were left in the empty night. I put my coat over him, chafed his hands and tried to warm his lips with my breath—nothing seemed any good. An awful memory came to me of the story of poor Art O'Neill, fugitive in those glens, frozen to death.

'I began to run blindly, for no reason, towards the trees.

'Out of the grove of trees a light shone; it was shining from an open door. I stumbled into the light and up the steps of a stone house; a grey-haired man stood there and a girl. "There's a man out there," I told them, "in the snow."

'They called servants and ran out with lanterns and a great dog followed them and found him and they brought him in.

'It took a long time to revive him, and his foot was lamed with frost-bite, but not much, and, but for that, he was soon well.

'We had come, I think, to the kindest folk in Ireland—the O'Byrnes of Glendasan. We must have travelled a dangerous way, they said, through Glenrigh, where King O'Toole is buried, past the grave of poor Art O'Neill—they knew the whole region—it was their own, and its histories, but they knew nothing about our guide.

'The Black and Tans caught nobody in the Glen.'

Amazed faces were turned to Michael as he ended his tale. Frank O'Carroll frowned but was silent; Max Barry, who is a rapacious historian, spoke eagerly: 'Art O'Neill? . . . Glenmalure! . . . Didn't Aodh Ruadh . . . wasn't it there?'

'Yes,' Una answered with glowing eyes, 'Aodh Ruadh O'Donal!—Red Hugh!'

Michael nodded, 'That is what Donal says.'

THE WOMAN WITHOUT MERCY

Maurice Walsh

*   *   *

Delgan walked the road all by himself, but Delgan was not lonely.
Behind him as he walked was a stupendous wide plain, and, a
million miles beyond the far-away curve of it, loomed the blue-grey
of mountains. And the same stupendous plain stretched away in
front of him, slowly lifting its grey-green like the sea, until, like
the sea, it rolled starkly over the horizon, beyond which were
no mountains, but splendid, serene white towers of cloud lifting
themselves out of the void beyond the world's edge. The immense
arch of the sky did not touch the horizon, but went unbelievably
beyond it on every hand, so that the towering white clouds seemed

to be in the foreground, and the plain, that went from horizon to horizon, no more than an unstable palm's-breadth thrust up into the voids of space. An imaginative man might have a fear that this plot of earth would at any moment reel and topple and fall forever through that void.

But Delgan did not walk as if he were on the edge of an abyss. His stride was long and supple, and in his own mind he towered into the sky and looked abroad over worlds. He was at one with sky and mountain and plain, and the austere morning light he evolved out of himself. But whatever he was in his own mind, in fact he was no more than a bright speck on that weary plain— that overawed, shallow crater of grey-green sloping up to the horizon and falling off into the deeps of the sky.

He was a tall man and a lean one, with a clean, set, blue-shaven face and black hair cut straight across above black brows and coming far down at the back of the neck. He was dressed in an orange tunic, gathered loosely at the waist by a green girdle, and leaving neck, arms, and legs brown and bare. A film of silken, black hair covered arms and legs, and as he strode forward one would have noticed that he was abnormally long of thigh and unduly short between bony knee and lean ankle. On his feet he wore leather sandals, and his toes were spaced widely. He carried a long, smooth staff of ash, but he did not use it as a staff. Sometimes it was over one shoulder and sometimes over the other, and again at the back of both and bending stiffly as his arms strained it, and now and then, when he was thinking, one end of it rested on the ground and his chin rested on the other over his clasped hands.

Delgan did not seem to be walking of any set purpose. He strolled, he loitered, he zig-zagged aimlessly. He gazed open-mouthed, narrow-eyed at the tremendous sky, wide-eyed at the ghost-mountains outside the world, frowningly at the dust of the road. He whispered words to himself, he whistled a bar of a tune, he hummed the verse of a song. Evidently the song was his own, for he smiled with some vanity, recited the verse with gusto, changed a word or two, shook his black head, and grew vacant-eyed with the inner travail of creation.

Though death doth dog my steps
With threat of hell hereafter,

74

I'll season life with love
And love with laughter.

That is what he declaimed, and thereafter frowned with the doubt of the creator.

'Death,' said he, to his toes, 'does not dog my steps, but only waits to welcome me at the end of pleasant roads, and hell has been quenched these thousand years. Moreover, I have small acquaintance with love, but, from what I have seen of it, it has many attributes, and laughter is not one of them. There is my brother Urnal now. If the tales be true, love has dealt hardly by him and by many good men through him.'

He strode on, still frowning, and the frown had not left his brow when he came suddenly on a fault in the plain and looked down into a little valley. He halted abruptly.

'Talk of the devil,' he said. 'There is Urnal himself and the woman with him.'

That valley was one of the surprises of that plain. From horizon to horizon stretched the plain, desolate, lifeless, infinitely austere: a smooth, unlined, slowly-lifting floor, where nothing moved but the cloud shadows, where nothing could cower away from the terrible immobility of the void. Yet across all its vast space it was seamed with little valleys such as this: shallow, narrow, verdant: pleasant places, with a stream loitering and hasting in the hollow, a cluster of shielings at every wimpling ford, hand-tilled gardens running up one slope and, running up the other, terraced vineyards facing the sun.

Delgan dipped down over the rim of the valley, and there was no longer a bright speck on the plain; there was nothing but grey-green grass undulating faintly in the wind, and cloud shadows running under the sun. Down there the very atmosphere was different: quiet instead of immobile, secure instead of uncaring, human instead of timeless, serene instead of austere. In an open space near the water, where a dark alder leant over a pool, sat a man and woman at food, and Delgan went directly to them by a path between the garden strips. The man rose to meet him. He was a younger man than Delgan, but he was as like him as any man could be: a little taller perhaps, a little wider in the shoulder, a little less lean of flank, but with the same swing and the same litheness. His black hair was cut in line with his black brows, and he has a dour, set, blue-shaven face. His tunic was orange also and girdled with green.

'At last, Urnal, I have found you,' said Delgan.

They placed affectionate hands on each other's shoulders, but in Urnal's touch there was, besides affection, some little hint of allegiance.

'I am glad you have found me, brother,' said Urnal in a slow voice that rumbled like a drum. 'Why, were you looking for me?'

'That can wait,' said Delgan lightly. 'I am looking now for breakfast.'

'Come, then,' invited Urnal. 'We have plenty.' He turned to where the woman sat, her back against the tree, and: 'Alor,' he said, 'this is my brother Delgan.'

'I knew that he was your brother,' said the woman. 'You are alike and yet unlike.'

'I have heard of you, Alor,' said Delgan. 'Men speak of you in all the valleys and in all the hills.'

'And I have heard much of Delgan,' said she.

'Only from his brother Urnal,' said Delgan.

'Only from your brother, indeed,' she admitted, 'but he speaks greatly of you.'

'That is my brother's way. But it is true that no one knows of Delgan, and that all the world knows of Urnal and his woman Alor.'

'I am not Urnal's woman,' said Alor quietly.

'And never will be,' said the heavy voice of Urnal.

'Let us eat,' said Delgan, and he and Urnal sat on the ground opposite Alor, who served them with brown bread and soya-bean cheese, and moved a great crystal jug of amber wine near their hands. As they ate they talked.

'It was up near the ice-line,' began Delgan, and, pausing, went off on an aside. 'Know ye that the ice-line is already down on the Cymbri, and I have been across to Eireann dryshod? The northern seas are all shallows these days.'

'I know,' said Urnal. 'All the people are drifting south.'

'Not all. There are some in Eireann who persist in living on the edge of the ice—men and women—all in the same tribe too, already eating flesh and evolving a god.'

'What else did you find at the ice-line?' questioned the woman.

'Tales of my brother Urnal and a woman Alor,' replied Delgan.

'If they were tales of blood they were true tales,' said Urnal.

'They were tales of great sword-work,' said Delgan.

'And why were you seeking your brother?' That woman was not afraid of any question.

'A man must do what he can for his own,' half-evaded Delgan, 'and I am Urnal's elder brother.'

He ate slowly, his eyes on the ground and his face very still. Urnal had finished eating, and he sat clasping his knees, his eyes on Alor, and his face a stone.

'When you are still,' said the woman, 'I find it hard to tell which is Urnal and which Delgan.'

'I am Urnal,' said Delgan.

'No. You have a face like doom, and Urnal the face of one already doomed.'

'You should know that,' said Delgan to the ground. He lifted his eyes and looked at his brother and his brother looked at him.

'I saw pale kings and princes too,
   Pale warriors, death-pale were they all;
Who cried, "The Woman Merciless
   Hath me in thrall."

'It was a singer of the old days, ten thousand years ago, that made that song,' said Delgan. 'He made many songs, they say, but only that and another live.'

He turned slow, musing eyes on Alor.

'Are you that woman without mercy?' he asked simply.

She flushed red to her red hair.

'I am only a woman,' she said, a little bitterly, 'and I use no wiles.'

And that protest Delgan did not question. He leant aside and put a hand over Urnal's clasped hands.

'What is your trouble, brother?' he asked, and there was grieving in his voice.

'I love that woman,' said Urnal heavily, 'and she does not know love at all.'

'But, indeed, I do,' denied the woman, but without heat. 'I shall know love when love comes. It is what I seek.'

'It is not wise to seek love,' chided Delgan. 'Why did you not stay in the place of women and let love seek you there?'

'I stayed in that place and the men came. There was no man amongst them. I do not think there is any man in all the world.'

'There is Urnal. He comes of a good stock. Is he not a fit mate for you?'

'The father of my son will not be Urnal,' was all she would say.

'Why not send him away then?'

She threw her hand towards Urnal in an expressive gesture.

'I cannot leave her, Delgan,' said that man, 'and she knows that I will not take what she will not give. She goes in many strange places, and to kill for her in her need is a great reward. Killing grows on one.'

'You know your rights, Alor,' said Delgan, not seeming to heed his brother. 'The people in all the twenty valleys would rid you of this man if you spoke the word.'

'I am no coward,' she said, 'and I am not yet afraid of Urnal, though he is a killer.'

'Are you not afraid at all?' wondered Delgan.

She looked at him, and as she looked his face froze, became stone, became implacable as fate, and a glaze went over his eyes. Her shoulders shrank a little as in a cold wind, and her eyes flickered, though they held.

'I am afraid of you,' she said simply.

'That fear will abide,' he said in a voice of brass, and turned to his brother.

'This woman will never be your woman,' he said. 'Killing does grow on one, brother. In time it ousts all other passions, even that of love, and in the end the killer is himself the killed. Until that end, Urnal, you will be but heaping pain on pain, for this woman has no mercy, and soon you, the killer, will have no mercy either. The woman is not to blame. She is older than all the tales, and all the great tales have been about her. All men desire her, and she, all desire, desires no one. Let her go her own road, brother, and let you and me go back to my father's house above the marshes of Rem. Come.'

'I will not come,' said Urnal slowly, but unhesitatingly. 'I am not unhappy, and I think that Alor is not unhappy either. I will go on until a better man kills me, or till Alor meets the man of her desire.'

'And him you will kill, too,' added Delgan.

Urnal made no reply to that.

'I was afraid that that would be the way of it,' said Delgan. 'I am too late for anything but the one thing,' and he rose to his feet and looked about him.

Two horses, long-tailed, rough-coated, medium-sized cayuses of the plains, saddled, but loose-girthed, grazed some distance up stream, and towards them Delgan walked slowly. Behind one saddle hung a long, straight sword in its sheath, and Delgan, with a quieting word to the horse, fingered the cross of the hilt. The horse swished a long tail and went on cropping.

'Drinker of blood,' he murmured, 'my father made you; guard you the life of his son Urnal, if you can, this day. Will you tell me if death is the only cure for some things—and I the killer or the killed? Will you tell me to go my own road out of this place and leave Urnal to his? You will say nothing that are always ready for your own work. Tell me, then, that Urnal is a man dogged by fate, running in a narrow groove, and not to be helped but by blow of blade. Tell me that I must kill the woman too, O sword! You will not. To kill her is not permitted, but some day the people, for their own sake, will decide that she must die. You and I will abide that day.'

He drew the sword, long and thin and with a blue sheen on it, and went back to the woman and his brother. He laid the sword at Urnal's feet.

'Brother,' he said quietly, 'I am taking the woman Alor.'

Urnal said nothing, but a small cold flame came into his eyes as they rested on the blade.

Delgan lifted his ashen staff and ran a hand down its smooth surface.

'You were splendid company on every road,' he said, 'and pleasant thoughts your aim. You whispered wisdom to me when you were under my chin, and when you whistled through the air you brought me the words of many a song. Go now on a voyage of your own.'

And javelin-like he threw it in the pool, where it dipped and floated and drifted aslant towards the shallows and the distant sea. Then he turned and strode down the valley to the hamlet by the ford.

The woman came across to Urnal and knelt by him.

'Kill that man for me,' she whispered in his ear.

Urnal had not changed his posture, and his eyes were still on the sword.

'I will not,' he told her. 'There is no need. Delgan is not a swordsman, and he does not yet desire you. I will but disarm him and send him on his road.'

Her breast pressed against his shoulder and her hands touched his neck.

'Kill him for me,' she whispered, 'and I will be the mother of your son.'

He lifted his head and looked at her, and the stone of his face quivered and broke.

*　　*　　*

When the people—it was a man's valley and there were no women—had assembled in the talk-ground above the ford Delgan made his demand.

'I have a quarrel,' said he, 'that only the sword can decide. Will the people lend me a sword?'

'Who are you and whom would you fight?' questioned the head-man.

'I am Urnal from Rem, of whom you may have heard, and I would fight the man who sits yonder with Alor.'

'There is dust on your feet,' said the other. 'Urnal rode in with Alor last evening and he had a sword hanging at his heel. He showed the young men some of his sword-play.'

'Yet I am Urnal.'

'And who is the other?'

'The other is already dead. He has no name any more.'

'So would Urnal speak,' said an old man, 'and you have the face of a killer. Why would you fight?'

'For the same reason that Urnal always fought.'

'What do Alor and the man say?' queried the head-man.

'Ask Alor and the man,' cried a young man impatiently. 'Give him a sword and we shall see if he can use it. Urnal of Rem can, and so can the man yonder, whoever he is.'

The head-man could not think of any more questions at that time.

'Bring the swords,' he said.

The impatient young man brought the swords. There were five of them shining wickedly on the grass.

'That is the best one,' pointed out the young man, 'and it is the best sword in the twenty valleys.'

Delgan lifted and hefted it.

'It is a good sword,' he agreed, 'but I will ride out of this valley with a better sword at my heel. Come now and see this one kill.'

He went up the valley, and all the people trooped after him and wondered.

The two blades clanged and held, and Urnal found that Delgan knew swording. He could not get his blade away from Delgan's— he never did get it away. The swords lifted into the air and screamed and writhed, and it was Urnal's arm that was forced up, and it was Urnal who yielded a step. The clinging blades came down in a wide swoop, and the blade of Delgan was inside the other. Close to the ground the steel wisps bent and writhed and groaned, and again it was Urnal who gave ground.

To the woman, leaning sombrely against the tree, weary of this work, to the half-circle of men intently watching, that sword-play looked no more than a supremely easy exhibition of skill—a small display of the art of engaging before the real work began. Instead of that it was a supreme effort of nerve and sinew. The tensed muscles stood out on forearms and on necks, the lithe bodies swayed and stiffened, the bony knees bowed and trembled, the sandal edges crushed the grass and bit deep into the firm soil, and the feet, that seemed to shift and leap with feather ease, met the ground with the stamp of iron. And always the blades remained locked.

After minutes the first blow was struck. It was the last blow also. At the very supreme moment of effort, before Urnal could yield the step he needed for balance, Delgan disengaged like lightning, and, as Urnal came in a stride, got in the blow he had played for: a sharp, crisp thud on the back of the neck. And on that instant Urnal was dead.

Delgan for a space looked down on the still body of his brother lying face-down at his feet. The people watched him silently, awesomely, and as one man they started when, suddenly, he swung on them. His face was frozen into something implacable as fate, a glaze was over his eyes, and his sword was held point forward in a stiff right hand.

'Who of you will take the woman Alor?' he challenged in a voice of brass.

No man there said one small word.

*　*　*

Alor and Delgan rode out over the rim of the valley, and his father's sword hung at Delgan's heel. The great plain smoothed itself out behind them, hiding beyond all guessing the little lives that moved subduedly within it. Delgan had come out of that valley a man changed in some subtle way, and, in his own mind, that change should have shaken the heavens. But the void had not changed at all. The cloud-shadows still ran, the wind blew forlornly out of desolate space, the void remained austerely immobile. It took no notice of Delgan; it took no notice of life; it was not concerned with man; it was concerned with Nothing.

THE VOYAGE OF MAILDUN

P. W. Joyce

*　　*　　*

There was once an illustrious man of the tribe of Owenaght of Ninus, Allil Ocar Aga by name, a goodly hero, and lord of his own tribe and territory. One time, when he was in his house unguarded, a fleet of plunderers landed on the coast, and spoiled his territory. The chief fled for refuge to the church of Dooclone; but the spoilers followed him thither, slew him, and burned the church over his head.

Not long after Allil's death, a son was born to him. The child's mother gave him the name of Maildun; and, wishing to conceal his birth, she brought him to the queen of that country, who was her dear friend. The queen took him to her, and gave out that he was her own child, and he was brought up with the king's sons, slept in the same cradle with them, and was fed from the same breast and from the same cup. He was a very lovely child; and the people who saw him thought it doubtful if there was any other child living at the time equally beautiful.

As he grew up to be a young man, the noble qualities of his mind gradually unfolded themselves. He was high-spirited and generous, and he loved all sorts of manly exercises. In ball-playing, in running and leaping, in throwing the stone, in chess-playing, in rowing, and in horse-racing, he surpassed all the youths that came to the king's palace, and won the palm in every contest.

One day, when the young men were at their games, a certain youth among them grew envious of Maildun; and he said, in an angry and haughty tone of voice:

'It is a cause of much shame to us that we have to yield in every game, whether of skill or of strength, whether on land or on water, to an obscure youth, of whom no one can tell who is his father or his mother, or what race or tribe he belongs to.'

On hearing this, Maildun ceased at once from play; for until that moment he believed that he was the son of the king of the Owenaght, and of the queen who had nursed him. And going anon to the queen, he told her what had happened, and he said to her—

'If I am not thy son, I will neither eat nor drink till thou tell me who my father and mother are.'

She tried to soothe him, and said, 'Why do you worry yourself searching after this matter? Give no heed to the words of this envious youth. Am I not a mother to you? And in all this country, is there any mother who loves her son better than I love you?'

He answered, 'All this is quite true; yet I pray thee let me know who my parents are.'

The queen then, seeing that he would not be put off, brought him to his mother, and put him into her hands. And when he had spoken with her, he asked her to tell him who his father was.

'You are bent on a foolish quest, my child,' she said; 'for even if you knew all about your father, the knowledge would bring neither advantage nor happiness to you; for he died before you were born.'

'Even so,' he replied, 'I wish to know who he was.'

So his mother told him the truth, saying, 'Your father was Allil Ocar Aga, of the tribe of Owenaght of Ninus.'

Maildun then set out for his father's territory; and his three foster brothers, namely, the king's three sons, who were noble and handsome youths like himself, went with him. When the people of his tribe found out that the strange youth was the son of their chief, whom the plunderers had slain years before, and when they were told that the three others were the king's sons, they gave them all a joyful welcome, feasting them, and showing them much honour; so that Maildun was made quite happy, and soon forgot all the abasement and trouble he had undergone.

Some time after this, it happened that a number of young people were in the churchyard of Dooclone—the same church in which Maildun's father had been slain—exercising themselves in casting a hand-stone. The game was to throw the stone clear over the charred roof of the church that had been burned; and Maildun was there contending among the others. A foul-tongued fellow named Brickna, a servant of the people who owned the church, was standing by; and he said to Maildun—

'It would better become you to avenge the man who was burned to death here, than to be amusing yourself casting a stone over his bare, burnt bones.'

'Who was he?' inquired Maildun.

'Allil Ocar Aga, your father,' replied the other.

'Who slew him?' asked Maildun.

'Plunderers from a fleet slew him and burned him in this church,' replied Brickna; 'and the same plunderers are still sailing in the same fleet.'

Maildun was disturbed and sad after hearing this. He dropped the stone that he held in his hand, folded his cloak round him, and buckled on his shield. And he left the company, and began to inquire of all he met, the road to the plunderers' ships. For a long time he could get no tidings of them; but at last some persons, who knew where the fleet lay, told him that it was a long way off, and that there was no reaching it except by sea.

Now Maildun was resolved to find out these plunderers, and to avenge on them the death of his father. So he went without delay into Corcomroe, to the druid Nuca, to seek his advice about building a curragh, and to ask also for a charm to protect him, both while building it, and while sailing on the sea afterwards.

The druid gave him full instructions. He told him the day he should begin to build his curragh, and the exact day on which he was to set out on his voyage; and he was very particular about the number of the crew, which, he said, was to be sixty chosen men, neither more nor less.

So Maildun built a large triple-hide curragh, following the druid's directions in every particular chose his crew of sixty, among whom were his two friends, Germane and Diuran Lekerd; and on the day appointed put out to sea.

When he had got only a very little way from the land, he saw his three foster brothers running down to the shore, signalling and calling out to him to return and take them on board; for they said they wished to go with him.

'We shall not turn back,' said Maildun; 'and you cannot come with us; for we have already got our exact number.'

'We will swim after you in the sea till we are drowned, if you do not return for us,' replied they; and so saying, the three plunged in and swam after the curragh.

When Maildun saw this, he turned his vessel towards them, and took them on board rather than let them be drowned.

They sailed that day and night, as well as the whole of next day, till darkness came on again; and at midnight they saw two small bare islands, with two great houses on them near the shore. When they drew near, they heard the sounds of merriment and laughter, and the shouts of revellers intermingled with the loud voices of warriors boasting of their deeds. And listening to catch the conversation, they heard one warrior say to another:

'Stand off from me, for I am a better warrior than thou; it was

I who slew Allil Ocar Aga, and burned Dooclone over his head; and no one has ever dared to avenge it on me. Thou hast never done a great deed like that!'

'Now surely,' said Germane and Diuran to Maildun, 'Heaven has guided our ship to this place! Here is an easy victory. Let us now sack this house, since God has revealed our enemies to us, and delivered them into our hands!'

While they were yet speaking, the wind arose, and a great tempest suddenly broke on them. And they were driven violently before the storm, all that night and a part of next day, into the great and boundless ocean; so that they saw neither the islands they had left nor any other land; and they knew not whither they were going.

Then Maildun said, 'Take down your sail and put by your oars, and let the curragh drift before the wind in whatsoever direction it pleases God to lead us;' which was done.

He then turned to his foster brothers, and said to them, 'This evil has befallen us because we took you into the curragh, thereby violating the druid's directions; for he forbade me to go to sea with more than sixty men for my crew, and we had that number before you joined us. Of a surety more evil will come of it.'

His foster brothers answered nothing to this, but remained silent.

For three days and three nights they saw no land. On the morning of the fourth day, while it was yet dark, they heard a sound to the north-east; and Germane said:

'This is the voice of the waves breaking on the shore.'

As soon as it was light they saw land and made towards it. While they were casting lots to know who should go and explore the country, they saw great flocks of ants coming down to the beach, each of them as large as a foal. The people judged by their numbers, and by their eager and hungry look, that they were bent on eating both ship and crew; so they turned their vessel round and sailed quickly away.

Again for three days and three nights they saw no land. But on the morning of the fourth day they heard the murmur of the waves on the beach; and as the day dawned, they saw a large high island, with terraces all round it, rising one behind another. On the terraces grew rows of tall trees, on which were perched great numbers of large, bright-coloured birds.

When the crew were about to hold council as to who should visit the island and see whether the birds were tame, Maildun himself offered to go. So he went with a few companions; and they viewed the island warily, but found nothing to hurt or alarm them; after which they caught great numbers of the birds and brought them to their ship.

They sailed from this, and on the fourth day discovered a large, sandy island, on which, when they came near, they saw a huge, fearful animal standing on the beach, and looking at them very attentively. He was somewhat like a horse in shape; but his legs were like the legs of a dog; and he had great, sharp claws of a blue colour.

Maildun, having viewed this monster for some time, liked not his look; and, telling his companions to watch him closely, for that he seemed bent on mischief, he bade the oarsmen row very slowly towards land.

The monster seemed much delighted when the ship drew nigh the shore, and gambolled and pranced about with joy on the beach, before the eyes of the voyagers; for he intended to eat the whole of them the moment they landed.

'He seems not at all sorry to see us coming,' said Maildun; 'but we must avoid him and put back from the shore.'

This was done. And when the animal observed them drawing off, he ran down in a great rage to the very water's edge, and digging up large, round pebbles with his sharp claws, he began to fling them at the vessel; but the crew soon got beyond his reach, and sailed into the open sea.

After sailing a long distance, they came in view of a broad, flat island. It fell to the lot of Germane to go and examine it, and he did not think the task a pleasant one. Then his friend Diuran said to him:

'I will go with you this time; and when next it falls to my lot to visit an island, you shall come with me.' So both went together.

They found the island very large; and some distance from the shore they came to a broad green race-course, in which they saw immense hoof-marks, the size of a ship's sail, or of a large dining-table. They found nut-shells, as large as helmets, scattered about; and although they could see no one, they observed all the marks and tokens that people of huge size were lately employed there at sundry kinds of work.

Seeing these strange signs, they became alarmed, and went and called their companions from the boat to view them. But the others, when they had seen them, were also struck with fear, and all quickly retired from the place and went on board their curragh.

When they had got a little way from the land, they saw dimly, as it were through a mist, a vast multitude of people on the sea; of gigantic size and demoniac look, rushing along the crests of the waves with great outcry. As soon as this shadowy host had landed, they went to the green, where they arranged a horse-race.

The horses were swifter than the wind; and as they pressed forward in the race, the multitudes raised a mighty shout like thunder, which reached the crew as if it were beside them. Maildun and his men, as they sat in their curragh, heard the strokes of the whips and the cries of the riders; and though the race was far off, they could distinguish the eager words of the spectators: 'Observe the grey horse!' 'See that chestnut horse!' 'Watch the horse with the white spots!' 'My horse leaps better than yours!'

After seeing and hearing these things, the crew sailed away from the island as quickly as they were able, into the open ocean, for they felt quite sure that the multitude they saw was a gathering of demons.

They suffered much from hunger and thirst this time, for they sailed a whole week without making land; but at the end of that time they came in sight of a high island, with a large and very splendid house on the beach near the water's edge. There were two doors—one turned inland, and the other facing the sea; and the door that looked towards the sea was closed with a great flat stone. In this stone was an opening, through which the waves, as they beat against the door every day, threw numbers of salmon into the house.

The voyagers landed, and went through the whole house without meeting any one. But they saw in one large room an ornamented couch, intended for the head of the house, and in each of the other rooms was a larger one for three members of the family: and there was a cup of crystal on a little table before each couch.

They found abundance of food and ale, and they ate and drank till they were satisfied, thanking God for having relieved them from hunger and thirst.

After leaving this, they suffered again from hunger, till they came to an island with a high hill round it on every side. A single apple tree grew in the middle, very tall and slender, and all its branches were in like manner exceedingly slender, and of wonderful length, so that they grew over the hill and down to the sea.

When the ship came near the island, Maildun caught one of the branches in his hand. For three days and three nights the ship coasted the island, and during all this time he held the branch, letting it slide through his hand, till on the third day he found a cluster of seven apples on the very end. Each of these apples supplied the travellers with food and drink for forty days and forty nights.

A beautiful island next came in view, in which they saw, at a distance, multitudes of large animals shaped like horses. The voyagers, as they drew near, viewed them attentively, and soon observed that one of them opened his mouth and bit a great piece out of the side of the animal that stood next him, bringing away skin and flesh. Immediately after, another did the same to the nearest of his fellows. And, in short, the voyagers saw that all the animals in the island kept worrying and tearing each other from time to time in this manner; so that the ground was covered far and wide with the blood that streamed from their sides.

The next island had a wall all round it. When they came near the shore, an animal of vast size, with a thick, rough skin, started up inside the wall, and ran round the island with the swiftness of the wind. When he had ended his race, he went to a high point, and standing on a large, flat stone, began to exercise himself according to his daily custom, in the following manner. He kept turning himself completely round and round in his skin, the bones and flesh moving, while the skin remained at rest.

When he was tired of this exercise, he rested a little; and he then began turning his skin continually round his body, down at one side and up at the other like a mill-wheel; but the bones and flesh did not move.

After spending some time at this sort of work, he started and ran round the island as at first, as if to refresh himself. He then went back to the same spot, and this time, while the skin that covered the lower part of his body remained without motion, he whirled the skin of the upper part round and round like the movement of a flat-lying millstone. And it was in this manner that he spent most of his time on the island.

Maildun and his people, after they had seen these strange doings, thought it better not to venture nearer. So they put out to sea in great haste. The monster, observing them about to fly, ran down to the beach to seize the ship; but finding that they had got out of his reach, he began to fling round stones at them with great force and an excellent aim. One of them struck Maildun's shield and went quite through it, lodging in the keel of the curragh; after which the voyagers got beyond his range and sailed away.

Not daring to land on this island, they turned away hurriedly, much disheartened, not knowing whither to turn or where to find a resting-place. They sailed for a long time, suffering much from hunger and thirst, and praying fervently to be relieved from their distress. At last, when they were beginning to sink into a state of despondency, being quite worn out with toil and hardship of every kind, they sighted land.

It was a large and beautiful island, with innumerable fruit trees scattered over its surface, bearing abundance of gold-coloured apples. Under the trees they saw herds of short, stout animals, of a bright red colour, shaped somewhat like pigs; but coming nearer, and looking more closely, they perceived with astonishment that the animals were all fiery, and that their bright colour was caused by the red flames which penetrated and lighted up their bodies.

The voyagers now observed several of them approach one of the trees in a body, and striking the trunk all together with their hind legs, they shook down some of the apples and ate them. In this manner the animals employed themselves every day, from early morning till the setting of the sun when they retired into deep caves, and were seen no more till next morning.

Numerous flocks of birds were swimming on the sea, all round the island. From morning till noon, they continued to swim away from the land, farther and farther out to sea; but at noon they turned round, and from that to sunset they swam back towards the shore. A little after sunset, when the animals had retired to their caves, the birds flocked in on the island, and spread themselves over it, plucking the apples from the trees and eating them.

Maildun proposed that they should land on the island, and gather some of the fruit, saying that it was not harder or more dangerous for them than for the birds; so two of the men were sent beforehand to examine the place. They found the ground hot under their feet, for the fiery animals, as they lay at rest, heated the earth all around and above their caves; but the two scouts persevered notwithstanding, and brought away some of the apples.

When morning dawned, the birds left the island and swam out to sea; and the fiery animals, coming forth from their caves, went among the trees as usual, and ate the apples till evening. The crew remained in their curragh all day; and as soon as the animals had gone into their caves for the night, and the birds had taken their place, Maildun landed with all his men. And they plucked the apples till morning, and brought them on board, till they had gathered as much as they could stow into their vessel.

After rowing for a long time, their store of apples failed them, and they had nothing to eat or drink; so that they suffered sorely under a hot sun, and their mouths and nostrils were filled with the briny smell of the sea. At last they came in sight of land—a little island with a large palace on it. Around the palace was a wall, white all over, without stain or flaw, as if it had been built of burnt lime, or carved out of one unbroken rock of chalk; and where it looked towards the sea it was so lofty that it seemed almost to reach the clouds.

The gate of this outer wall was open, and a number of fine houses, all snowy white, were ranged round on the inside, enclosing a level court in the middle, on which all the houses opened. Maildun and his people entered the largest of them, and walked through several rooms without meeting with any one. But on reaching the principal apartment, they saw in it a small cat, playing among a number of low, square, marble pillars, which stood ranged in a row; and his play was, leaping continually from the top of one pillar to the top of another. When the men entered the room, the cat looked at them for a moment, but returned to his play anon, and took no further notice of them.

Looking now to the room itself, they saw three rows of precious jewels ranged round the wall from one door-jamb to the other. The first was a row of brooches of gold and silver, with their pins fixed in the wall, and their heads outwards; the second, a row of torques of gold and silver; and the third, a row of great swords, with hilts of gold and silver.

Round the room were arranged a number of couches, all pure white and richly ornamented. Abundant food of various kinds was spread on tables, among which they observed a boiled ox and a roast hog; and there were many large drinking-horns, full of good, intoxicating ale.

'Is it for us that this food has been prepared?' said Maildun to the cat.

The cat, on hearing the question, ceased from playing, and looked at him; but he recommenced his play immediately. Whereupon Maidun told his people that the dinner was meant for them; and they all sat down, and ate and drank till they were satisfied, after which they rested and slept on the couches.

When they awoke, they poured what was left of the ale into one vessel; and they gathered the remnants of the food to bring them away. As they were about to go, Maildun's eldest foster brother asked him:

'Shall I bring one of those large torques away with me?'

'By no means,' said Maildun; 'it is well that we have got food and rest. Bring nothing away, for it is certain that this house is not left without some one to guard it.'

The young man, however, disregarding Maildun's advice, took down one of the torques and brought it away. But the cat followed him, and overtook him in the middle of the court, and, springing on him like a blazing, fiery arrow, he went through his body, and reduced it in a moment to a heap of ashes. He then returned to the room, and, leaping up on one of the pillars, sat upon it.

Maildun turned back, bringing the torque with him, and, approaching the cat, spoke some soothing words; after which he put the torque back to the place from which it had been taken. Having done this, he collected the ashes of his foster brother, and, bringing them to the shore, cast them into the sea. They all then went on board the curragh, and continued their voyage, grieving for their lost companion, but thanking God for His many mercies to them.

On the morning of the third day, they came to another island, which was divided into two parts by a wall of brass running across the middle. They saw two great flocks of sheep, one on each side of the wall; and all those at one side were black, while those at the other side were white.

A very large man was employed in dividing and arranging the sheep; and he often took up a sheep and threw it with much ease over the wall from one side to the other. When he threw over a white sheep among the black ones, it became black immediately; and in like manner, when he threw a black sheep over, it was instantly changed to white.

The travellers were very much alarmed on witnessing these doings; and Maildun said:

'It is very well that we know so far. Let us now throw something on shore, to see whether it also will change colour; if it does, we shall avoid the island.'

So they took a branch with black-coloured bark and threw it towards the white sheep, and no sooner did it touch the ground than it became white. They then threw a white-coloured branch on the side of the black sheep, and in a moment it turned black.

'It is very lucky for us,' said Maildun, 'that we did not land on the island, for doubtless our colour would have changed like the colour of the branches.'

So they put about with much fear, and sailed away.

On the third day, they came in view of a large, broad island, on which they saw a herd of gracefully shaped swine; and they killed one small porkling for food. Towards the centre rose a high mountain, which they resolved to ascend, in order to view the island; and Germane and Diuran Lekerd were chosen for this task.

When they had advanced some distance towards the mountain, they came to a broad, shallow river; and sitting down on the bank to rest, Germane dipped the point of his lance into the water, which instantly burned off the top, as if the lance had been thrust into a furnace. So they went no farther.

On the opposite side of the river, they saw a herd of animals like great hornless oxen, all lying down; and a man of gigantic size near them: and Germane began to strike his spear against his shield, in order to rouse the cattle.

'Why are you frightening the poor young calves in that manner?' demanded the big shepherd, in a tremendous voice.

Germane, astonished to find that such large animals were nothing more than calves, instead of answering the question, asked the big man where the mothers of those calves were.

'They are on the side of yonder mountain,' he replied.

Germane and Diuran waited to hear no more; but, returning to their companions, told them all they had seen and heard; after which the crew embarked and left the island.

The next island they came to, which was not far off from the last, had a large mill on it; and near the door stood the miller, a huge-bodied, strong, burly man. They saw numberless crowds of men and horses laden with corn, coming towards the mill; and when their corn was ground they went away towards the west. Great herds of all kinds of cattle covered the plain as far as the eye could reach, and among them many wagons laden with every kind of wealth that is produced on the ridge of the world. All these the miller put into the mouth of his mill to be ground; and all, as they came forth, went westwards.

Maildun and his people now spoke to the miller, and asked him the name of the mill, and the meaning of all they had seen on the island. And he, turning quickly towards them, replied in few words:

'This mill is called the Mill of Inver-tre-Kenand, and I am the miller of hell. All the corn and all the riches of the world that men are dissatisfied with, or which they complain of in any way, are sent here to be ground; and also every precious article, and every kind of wealth, which men try to conceal from God. All these I grind in the Mill of Inver-tre-Kenand, and send them afterwards away to the west.'

He spoke no more, but turned round and busied himself again with his mill. And the voyagers, with much wonder and awe in their hearts, went to their curragh and sailed away.

After leaving this, they had not been long sailing when they discovered another large island, with a great multitude of people on it. They were all black, both skin and clothes, with black headdresses also; and they kept walking about, sighing and weeping and wringing their hands, without the least pause or rest.

It fell to the lot of Maildun's second foster brother to go and examine the island. And when he went among the people, he also grew sorrowful, and fell to weeping and wringing his hands, with the others. Two of the crew were sent to bring him back; but they were unable to find him among the mourners; and, what was worse, in a little time they joined the crowd, and began to weep and lament like all the rest.

Maildun then chose four men to go and bring back the others by force, and he put arms in their hands, and gave them these directions:

'When you land on the island, fold your mantles round your faces, so as to cover your mouths and noses, that you may not breathe the air of the country; and look neither to the right nor to the left, neither at the earth nor at the sky, but fix your eyes on your own men till you have laid hands on them.'

They did exactly as they were told, and having come up with their two companions, namely, those who had been sent after Maildun's foster brother, they seized them and brought them back by force. But the other they could not find. When these two were asked what they had seen on the island, and why they began to weep, their only reply was:

'We cannot tell; we only know that we did what we saw the others doing.'

And after this the voyagers sailed away from the island, leaving Maildun's second foster brother behind.

The next was a high island, divided into four parts by four walls meeting in the centre. The first was a wall of gold; the second, a wall of silver; the third, a wall of copper; and the fourth, a wall of crystal. In the first of the four divisions were kings; in the second, queens; in the third, youths; and in the fourth, young maidens.

When the voyagers landed, one of the maidens came to meet them, and leading them forward to a house, gave them food. This food, which she dealt out to them from a small vessel, looked like cheese, and whatever taste pleased each person best, that was the taste he found on it. And after they had eaten till they were satisfied, they slept in a sweet sleep, as if gently intoxicated, for three days and three nights. When they awoke on the third day, they found themselves in their curragh on the open sea; and there was no appearance in any direction either of the maiden or of the island.

They came now to a small island, with a palace on it, having a copper chain in front, hung all over with a number of little silver bells. Straight before the door there was a fountain, spanned by a bridge of crystal, which led to the palace. They walked towards the bridge, meaning to cross it, but every time they stepped on it they fell backwards flat on the ground.

After some time, they saw a very beautiful young woman coming out of the palace, with a pail in her hand; and she lifted a crystal slab from the bridge, and, having filled her vessel from the fountain, she went back into the palace.

'This woman has been sent to keep house for Maildun,' said Germane.

'Maildun indeed!' said she, as she shut the door after her.

After this they began to shake the copper chain, and the tinkling of the silver bells was so soft and melodious that the voyagers gradually fell into a gentle, tranquil sleep, and slept so till next morning. When they awoke, they saw the same young woman coming forth from the palace, with the pail in her hand; and she lifted the crystal slab as before, filled her vessel, and returned into the palace.

'This woman has certainly been sent to keep house for Maildun,' said Germane.

'Wonderful are the powers of Maildun!' said she, as she shut the door of the court behind her.

They stayed in this place for three days and three nights, and each morning the maiden came forth in the same manner, and filled her pail. On the fourth day, she came towards them, splendidly and beautifully dressed, with her bright yellow hair bound by a circlet of gold, and wearing silver-work shoes on her small, white feet. She had a white mantle over her shoulders, which was fastened in front by a silver brooch studded with gold; and under all, next her soft, snow-white skin, was a garment of fine white silk.

'My love to you, Maildun, and to your companions,' she said; and she mentioned them all, one after another, calling each by his own proper name. 'My love to you,' said she. 'We knew well that you were coming to our island, for your arrival has long been foretold to us.'

Then she led them to a large house standing by the sea, and she caused the curragh to be drawn high up on the beach. They found in the house a number of couches, one of which was intended for Maildun alone, and each of the others for three of his people. The woman then gave them, from one vessel, food which was like cheese; first of all ministering to Maildun, and then giving a triple share to every three of his companions; and whatever taste each man wished for, that was the taste he found on it. She then lifted the crystal slab at the bridge, filled her pail, and dealt out drink to them; and she knew exactly how much to give, both of food and of drink, so that each had enough and no more.

'This woman would make a fit wife for Maildun,' said his people. But while they spoke, she went from them with her pail in her hand.

When she was gone, Maildun's companions said to him, 'Shall we ask this maiden to become thy wife?'

He answered, 'What advantage will it be to you to ask her?'

She came next morning, and they said to her, 'Why dost thou not stay here with us? Wilt thou make friendship with Maildun; and wilt thou take him for thy husband?'

She replied that she and all those that lived on the island were forbidden to marry with the sons of men; and she told them that she could not disobey, as she knew not what sin or transgression was.

She then went from them to her house; and on the next morning, when she returned, and after she had ministered to them as usual, till they were satisfied with food and drink, and were become cheerful, they spoke the same words to her.

'Tomorrow,' she replied, 'you will get an answer to your question;' and so saying, she walked towards her house, and they went to sleep on their couches.

When they awoke next morning, they found themselves lying in their curragh on the sea, beside a great high rock; and when they looked about, they saw neither the woman, nor the palace of the crystal bridge, nor any trace of the island where they had been sojourning.

One night, soon after leaving this, they heard in the distance, towards the north-east, a confused murmur of voices, as if from a great number of persons singing psalms. They followed the direction of the sound, in order to learn from what it proceeded; and at noon the next day, they came in view of an island, very hilly and lofty. It was full of birds, some black, some brown, and some speckled, who were all shouting and speaking with human voices; and it was from them that the great clamour came.

At a little distance from this they found another small island, with many trees on it, some standing singly, and some in clusters, on which were perched great numbers of birds. They also saw an aged man on the island, who was covered thickly all over with long, white hair, and wore no other dress. And when they landed, they spoke to him, and asked him who he was and what race he belonged to.

'I am one of the men of Erin,' he replied. 'On a certain day, a long, long time ago, I embarked in a small curragh, and put out to sea on a pilgrimage; but I had got only a little way from shore, when my curragh became very unsteady, as if it were about to overturn. So I returned to land, and, in order to steady my boat, I placed under my feet at the bottom, a number of green surface sods, cut from one of the grassy fields of my own country, and began my voyage anew. Under the guidance of God, I arrived at this spot; and He fixed the sods in the sea for me, so that they formed a little island. At first I had barely room to stand; but every year, from that time to the present, the Lord has added one foot to the length and breadth of my island, till in the long lapse of ages it has grown to its present size. And on one day in each year, He has caused a single tree to spring up, till the island has become covered with trees. Moreover, I am so old that my body, as you see, has become covered with long, white hair, so that I need no other dress.

'And the birds that ye see on the trees,' he continued, 'these are the souls of my children, and of all my descendants, both men and women, who are sent to this little island to abide with me according as they die in Erin. God has caused a well of ale to spring up for us on the island: and every morning the angels bring me half a cake, a slice of fish, and a cup of ale from the well; and in the evening the same allowance of food and ale is dealt out to each man and woman of my people. And it is in this manner that we live, and shall continue to live till the end of the world; for we are all awaiting here the day of judgment.'

Maildun and his companions were treated hospitably on the island by the old pilgrim for three days and three nights; and when they were taking leave of him, he told them that they should all reach their own country except one man.

When they had been for a long time tossed about on the waters, they saw land in the distance. On approaching the shore, they heard the roaring of a great bellows, and the thundering sound of smiths' hammers striking a large glowing mass of iron on an anvil; and every blow seemed to Maildun as loud as if a dozen men had brought down their sledges all together.

When they had come a little nearer, they heard the big voices of the smiths in eager talk.

'Are they near?' asked one.

'Hush! silence!' says another.

'Who are they that you say are coming?' inquired a third.

'Little fellows, that are rowing towards our shore in a pigmy boat,' says the first.

When Maildun heard this, he hastily addressed the crew:

'Put back at once, but do not turn the curragh: reverse the sweep of your oars, and let her move stern forward, so that those giants may not perceive that we are flying!'

The crew at once obey, and the boat begins to move away from the shore, stern forward, as he had commanded.

The first smith again spoke. 'Are they near enough to the shore?' said he to the man who was watching.

'They seem to be at rest,' answered the other; 'for I cannot perceive that they are coming closer, and they have not turned their little boat to go back.'

In a short time the first smith asks again, 'What are they doing now?'

'I think,' said the watcher, 'they are flying; for it seems to me that they are now farther off than they were a while ago.'

At this the first smith rushed out of the forge—a huge, burly giant—holding, in the tongs which he grasped in his right hand, a vast mass of iron sparkling and glowing from the furnace; and, running down to the shore with long, heavy strides, he flung the redhot mass with all his might after the curragh. It fell a little short, and plunged down just near the prow, causing the whole sea to hiss and boil and heave up around the boat. But they plied their oars, so that they quickly got beyond his reach, and sailed out into the open ocean.

After a time, they came to a sea like green crystal. It was so calm and transparent that they could see the sand at the bottom quite clearly, sparkling in the sunlight. And in this sea they saw neither monsters, nor ugly animals, nor rough rocks; nothing but the clear water and the sunshine and the bright sand. For a whole day they sailed over it, admiring its splendour and beauty.

After leaving this they entered on another sea, which seemed like a clear, thin cloud; and it was so transparent, and appeared so light, that they thought at first it would not bear up the weight of the curragh.

Looking down, they could see, beneath the clear water, a beautiful country, with many mansions surrounded by groves and woods. In one place was a single tree; and, standing on its branches, they saw an animal fierce and terrible to look upon.

Round about the tree was a great herd of oxen grazing, and a man stood near to guard them, armed with shield and spear and sword; but when he looked up and saw the animal on the tree, he turned anon and fled with the utmost speed. Then the monster stretched forth his neck, and, darting his head downward, plunged his fangs into the back of the largest ox of the whole herd, lifted him off the ground into the tree, and swallowed him down in the twinkling of an eye; whereupon the whole herd took to flight.

When Maildun and his people saw this, they were seized with great terror; for they feared they should not be able to cross the sea over the monster, on account of the extreme mist-like thinness of the water; but after much difficulty and danger they got across it safely.

When they came to the next island, they observed with astonishment that the sea rose up over it on every side, steep and high, standing, as it were, like a wall all round it. When the people of the island saw the voyagers, they rushed hither and thither, shouting, 'There they are, surely! There they come again for another spoil!'

Then Maildun's people saw great numbers of men and women, all shouting and driving vast herds of horses, cows, and sheep. A woman began to pelt the crew from below with large nuts; she flung them so that they alighted on the waves round the boat, where they remained floating; and the crew gathered great quantities of them and kept them for eating.

When they turned to go away, the shouting ceased; and they heard one man calling aloud, 'Where are they now?' and another answering him, 'They are gone away!'

From what Maildun saw and heard at this island, it is likely that it had been foretold to the people that their country should some day be spoiled by certain marauders; and that they thought Maildun and his men were the enemies they expected.

On the next island they saw a very wonderful thing, namely, a great stream of water which, gushing up out of the strand, rose into the air in the form of a rainbow, till it crossed the whole island and came down on the strand at the other side. They walked under it without getting wet; and they hooked down from it many large salmon. Great quantities of salmon of a very great size fell also out of the water over their heads down on the ground; so that the whole island smelled of fish, and it became troublesome to gather them on account of their abundance.

From the evening of Sunday till the evening of Monday, the stream never ceased to flow, and never changed its place, but remained spanning the island like a solid arch of water. Then the voyagers gathered the largest of the salmon, till they had as much as the curragh would hold; after which they sailed out into the great sea.

The next thing they found after this was an immense silver pillar standing in the sea. It had eight sides, each of which was the width of an oar-stroke of the curragh, so that its whole circumference was eight oar-strokes. It rose out of the sea without any land or earth about it, nothing but the boundless ocean; and they could not see its base deep down in the water, neither were they able to see the top on account of its vast height.

A silver net hung from the top down to the very water, extending far out at one side of the pillar; and the meshes were so large that the curragh in full sail went through one of them. When they were passing through it, Diuran struck the mesh with the edge of his spear, and with the blow cut a large piece off it.

'Do not destroy the net,' said Maildun; 'for what we see is the work of great men.'

'What I have done,' answered Diuran, 'is for the honour of my God, and in order that the story of our adventures may be more readily believed; and I shall lay this silver as an offering on the altar of Armagh, if I ever reach Erin.'

That piece of silver weighed two ounces and a half, as it was reckoned afterwards by the people of the church of Armagh.

After this they heard some one speaking on the top of the pillar, in a loud, clear, glad voice; but they knew neither what he said, nor in what language he spoke.

The island they saw after this was named Encos;[1] and it was so called because it was supported by a single pillar in the middle. They rowed all round it, seeking how they might get into it; but could find no landing-place. At the foot of the pillar, however, down deep in the water, they saw a door securely closed and locked, and they judged that this was the way into the island. They called aloud, to find out if any persons were living there; but they got no reply. So they left it, and put out to sea once more.

The next island they reached was very large. On one side rose a lofty, smooth, heath-clad mountain, and all the rest of the island was a grassy plain. Near the sea-shore stood a great high palace, adorned with carvings and precious stones, and strongly fortified with a high rampart all round. After landing, they went towards the palace, and sat to rest on the bench before the gateway leading through the outer rampart; and, looking in through the open door, they saw a number of beautiful young maidens in the court.

After they had sat for some time, a rider appeared at a distance, coming swiftly towards the palace; and on a near approach, the travellers perceived that it was a lady, young and beautiful and richly dressed. She wore a blue, rustling silk head-dress; a silver-fringed purple cloak hung from her shoulders; her gloves were embroidered with gold thread; and her feet were laced becomingly in close-fitting scarlet sandals. One of the maidens came out and held her horse, while she dismounted and entered the palace; and

1 Encos means 'one foot'.

soon after she had gone in, another of the maidens came towards Maildun and his companions and said:

'You are welcome to this island. Come into the palace; the queen has sent me to invite you, and is waiting to receive you.'

They followed the maiden into the palace; and the queen bade them welcome, and received them kindly. Then, leading them into a large hall in which a plentiful dinner was laid out, she bade them sit down and eat. A dish of choice food and a crystal goblet of wine were placed before Maildun; while a single dish and a single drinking-bowl, with a triple quantity of meat and drink, were laid before each three of his companions. And having eaten and drunk till they were satisfied, they went to sleep on soft couches till morning.

Next day, the queen addressed Maildun and his companions:

'Stay now in this country, and do not go a-wandering any longer over the wide ocean from island to island. Old age or sickness shall never come upon you; but you shall be always as young as you are at present, and you shall live for ever a life of ease and pleasure.'

'Tell us,' said Maildun, 'how you pass your life here.'

'That is no hard matter,' answered the queen. 'The good king who formerly ruled over this island was my husband, and these fair young maidens that you see are our children. He died after a long reign, and as he left no son, I now reign, the sole ruler of the island. And every day I go to the Great Plain, to administer justice and to decide causes among my people.'

'Wilt thou go from us today?' asked Maildun.

'I must needs go even now,' she replied, 'to give judgments among the people; but as to you, you will all stay in this house till I return in the evening, and you need not trouble yourselves with any labour or care.'

They remained in that island during the three months of winter. And these three months appeared to Maildun's companions as long as three years, for they began to have an earnest desire to return to their native land. At the end of that time, one of them said to Maildun:

'We have been a long time here; why do we not return to our own country?'

'What you say is neither good nor sensible,' answered Maildun, 'for we shall not find in our own country anything better than we have here.'

But this did not satisfy his companions, and they began to murmur loudly. 'It is quite clear,' said they, 'that Maildun loves the queen of this island; and as this is so, let him stay here; but as for us, we will return to our own country.'

Maildun, however, would not consent to remain after them, and he told them that he would go away with them.

Now, on a certain day, not long after this conversation, as soon as the queen had gone to the Great Plain to administer justice, according to her daily custom, they got their curragh ready and put out to sea. They had not gone very far from land when the queen came riding towards the shore; and, seeing how matters stood, she went into the palace and soon returned with a ball of thread in her hand.

Walking down to the water's edge, she flung the ball after the curragh, but held the end of the thread in her hand. Maildun caught the ball as it was passing, and it clung to his hand; and the queen, gently pulling the thread towards her, drew back the curragh to the very spot from which they had started in the little harbour. And when they had landed, she made them promise that if ever this happened again, some one should always stand up in the boat and catch the ball.

The voyagers abode on the island, much against their will, for nine months longer. For every time they attempted to escape, the queen brought them back by means of the clew, as she had done at first, Maildun always catching the ball.

At the end of the nine months, the men held council, and this is what they said:

'We know now that Maildun does not wish to leave the island; for he loves this queen very much, and he catches the ball whenever we try to escape, in order that we may be brought back to the palace.'

Maildun replied, 'Let some one else attend to the ball next time, and let us try whether it will cling to his hand.'

They agreed to this, and, watching their opportunity, they again put off towards the open sea. The queen arrived, as usual, before they had gone very far and flung the ball after them as before. Another man of the crew caught it, and it clung as firmly to his hand as to Maildun's; and the queen began to draw the curragh towards the shore. But Diuran, drawing his sword, cut off the man's hand, which fell with the ball into the sea; and the men gladly plying their oars, the curragh resumed her outward voyage.

When the queen saw this, she began to weep and lament, wringing her hands and tearing her hair with grief; and her maidens also began to weep and cry aloud and clap their hands, so that the whole palace was full of grief and lamentation. But none the less did the men bend to their oars, and the curragh sailed away; and it was in this manner that the voyagers made their escape from the island.

They were now a long time tossed about on the great billows, when at length they came in view of an island with many trees on it. These trees were somewhat like hazels, and they were laden with a kind of fruit which the voyagers had not seen before, extremely large, and not very different in appearance from apples, except that they had a rough, berry-like rind.

After the crew had plucked all the fruit off one small tree, they cast lots who should try them, and the lot fell on Maildun. So he took some of them, and, squeezing the juice into a vessel, drank it. It threw him into a sleep of intoxication so deep that he seemed to be in a trance rather than in a natural slumber, without breath or motion, and with the red foam on his lips. And from that hour till the same hour next day, no one could tell whether he was living or dead.

When he awoke next day, he bade his people to gather as much of the fruit as they could bring away with them; for the world, as he told them, never produced anything of such surpassing goodness. They pressed out the juice of the fruit till they had filled all their vessels; and so powerful was it to produce intoxication and sleep, that, before drinking it, they had to mix a large quantity of water with it to moderate its strength.

The island they came to next was larger than most of those they had seen. On one side grew a wood of yew trees and great oaks; and on the other side was a grassy plain, with one small lake in the midst. A noble-looking house stood on the near part of the plain, with a small church not far off; and numerous flocks of sheep browsed over the whole island.

The travellers went to the church, and found in it a hermit, with snow-white beard and hair, and all the other marks of great old age. Maildun asked who he was, and whence he had come.

He replied, 'I am one of the fifteen people, who, following the example of our master, Brendan of Birra, sailed on a pilgrimage out into the great ocean. After many wanderings, we settled on this island, where we lived for a long time; but my companions died one after another, and of all who came hither, I alone am left.'

The old pilgrim then showed them Brendan's satchel, which he and his companions had brought with them on their pilgrimage; and Maildun kissed it, and all bowed down in veneration before it. And he told them that as long as they remained there, they might eat of the sheep and of the other food of the island; but to waste nothing.

One day, as they were seated on a hill, gazing out over the sea, they saw what they took to be a black cloud coming towards them from the south-west. They continued to view it very closely as it came nearer and nearer; and at last they perceived with amazement that it was an immense bird, for they saw quite plainly the slow, heavy flapping of his wings. When he reached the island, he alighted on a little hillock over the lake; and they felt no small alarm, for they thought, on account of his vast size, that if he saw them, he might seize them in his talons, and carry them off over the sea. So they hid themselves under trees and in the crannies of rocks; but they never lost sight of the bird, for they were bent on watching his movements.

He appeared very old, and he held in one claw a branch of a tree, which he had brought with him over the sea, larger and heavier than the largest full-grown oak. It was covered with fresh, green leaves, and was heavily laden with clusters of fruit, red and rich-looking like grapes, but much larger.

He remained resting for a time on the hill, being much wearied after his flight, and at last he began to eat the fruit off the branch. After watching him for some time longer, Maildun ventured warily towards the hillock, to see whether he was inclined to mischief; but the bird showed no disposition to harm him. This emboldened the others, and they all followed their chief.

The whole crew now marched in a body round the bird, headed by Maildun, with their shields raised; and as he still made no stir, one of the men, by Maildun's directions, went straight in front of him, and brought away some of the fruit from the branch which he still held in his talons. But the bird went on plucking and eating his fruit, and never took the least notice.

On the evening of that same day, as the men sat looking over the sea to the south-west, where the great bird first appeared to them, they saw in the distance two others, quite as large, coming slowly towards them from the very same point. On they came, flying at a vast height, nearer and nearer, till at last they swooped down and alighted on the hillock in front of the first bird, one on each side.

Although they were plainly much younger than the other, they seemed very tired, and took a long rest. Then, shaking their wings, they began picking the old bird all over, body, wings, and head, plucking out the old feathers and the decayed quill points, and smoothing down his plumage with their great beaks. After this had gone on for some time, the three began plucking the fruit off the branch, and they ate till they were satisfied.

Next morning, the two birds began at the very same work, picking and arranging the feathers of the old bird as before; and at midday they ceased, and began again to eat the fruit, throwing the stones and what they did not eat of the pulp, into the lake, till the water became red like wine. After this the old bird plunged into the lake and remained in it, washing himself, till evening, when he again flew up on the hillock, but perched on a different part of it, to avoid touching and defiling himself with the old feathers and the other traces of age and decay, which the younger birds had removed from him.

On the morning of the third day, the two younger birds set about arranging his feathers for the third time; and on this occasion they applied themselves to their task in a manner much more careful and particular than before, smoothing the plumes with the nicest touches, and arranging them in beautiful lines and glossy tufts and ridges. And so they continued without the least pause till midday, when they ceased. Then, after resting for a little while, they opened their great wings, rose into the air, and flew away swiftly towards the south-west, till the men lost sight of them in the distance.

Meantime the old bird, after the others had left, continued to smooth and plume his feathers till evening; then, shaking his wings, he rose up, and flew three times round the island, as if to

try his strength. And now the men observed that he had lost all
the appearances of old age: his feathers were thick and glossy, his
head was erect and his eye bright, and he flew with quite as much
power and swiftness as the others. Alighting for the last time
on the hillock, after resting a little, he rose again, and turning
his flight after the other two, to the point from which he had
come, he was soon lost to view, and the voyagers saw no more
of him.

It now appeared very clear to Maildun and his companions that
this bird had undergone a renewal of youth from old age, according
to the word of the prophet, which says, 'Thy youth shall be
renewed as the eagle.' Diuran, seeing this great wonder, said to
his companions:

'Let us also bathe in the lake, and we shall obtain a renewal of
youth like the bird.'

But they said, 'Not so, for the bird has left the poison of his old
age and decay in the water.'

Diuran, however, would have his own way; and he told them
he was resolved to try the virtue of the water, and that they might
follow his example or not, whichever they pleased. So he plunged
in and swam about for some time, after which he took a little of
the water and mixed it in his mouth; and in the end he swallowed
a small quantity. He then came out perfectly sound and whole;
and he remained so ever after, for as long as he lived he never
lost a tooth or had a grey hair, and he suffered not from disease
or bodily weakness of any kind. But none of the others ventured
in.

The voyagers, having remained long enough on this island,
stored in their curragh a large quantity of the flesh of the sheep;
and after bidding farewell to the ancient cleric, they sought the
ocean once more.

They next came to an island with a great plain extending over its
whole surface. They saw a vast multitude of people on it, engaged
in sundry youthful games, and all continually laughing. The
voyagers cast lots who should go to examine the island; and the
lot fell upon Maildun's third foster brother.

The moment he landed he went among the others and joined
in their pastimes and in their laughter, as if he had been among
them all his life. His companions waited for him a very long time,

but were afraid to venture to land after him; and at last, as there seemed no chance of his returning, they left him and sailed away.

They came now to a small island with a high wall of fire all round it, and there was a large open door in the wall at one side near the sea. They sailed backward and forward many times, and always paused before the door; for whenever they came right in front of it, they could see almost the whole island through it.

And this is what they saw: A great number of people, beautiful and glorious-looking, wearing rich garments adorned and radiant all over, feasting joyously, and drinking from embossed vessels of red gold which they held in their hands. The voyagers heard also their cheerful, festive songs; and they marvelled greatly, and their hearts were full of gladness at all the happiness they saw and heard. But they did not venture to land.

A little time after leaving this, they saw something a long way off towards the south, which at first they took to be a large white bird floating on the sea, and rising and falling with the waves; but on turning their curragh towards it for a nearer view, they found that it was a man. He was very old, so old that he was covered all over with long, white hair, which grew from his body; and he was standing on a broad, bare rock, and kept continually throwing himself on his knees, and never ceased praying.

When they saw that he was a holy man, they asked and received his blessing; after which they began to converse with him; and they inquired who he was, and how he had come to that rock. Then the old man gave them the following account:

'I was born and bred in the island of Tory.[1] When I grew up to be a man, I was cook to the brotherhood of the monastery; and a wicked cook I was; for every day I sold part of the food intrusted to me, and secretly bought many choice and rare things with the money. Worse even than this I did; I made secret passages underground into the church and into the houses belonging to it, and I stole from time to time great quantities of golden vestments, book-covers adorned with brass and gold, and other holy and precious things.

---

1 Tory Island, off the coast of Donegal, where there was a monastery dedicated to St Columkille.

'I soon became very rich, and had my rooms filled with costly couches, with clothes of every colour, both linen and woollen, with brazen pitchers and caldrons, and with brooches and armlets of gold. Nothing was wanting in my house, of furniture and ornament, that a person in a high rank of life might be expected to have; and I became very proud and overbearing.

'One day, I was sent to dig a grave for the body of a rustic that had been brought from the mainland to be buried on the island. I went and fixed on a spot in the little graveyard; but as soon as I had set to work, I heard a voice speaking down deep in the earth beneath my feet:

'"Do not dig this grave!"

'I paused for a moment, startled; but, recovering myself, I gave no further heed to the mysterious words, and again I began to dig. The moment I did so, I heard the same voice, even more plainly than before:

'"Do not dig this grave! I am a devout and holy person, and my body is lean and light; do not put the heavy, pampered body of that sinner down upon me!"

'But I answered, in the excess of my pride and obstinacy, "I will certainly dig this grave; and I will bury this body down on you!"

'"If you put that body down on me, the flesh will fall off your bones, and you will die, and be sent to the infernal pit at the end of three days; and, moreover, the body will not remain where you put it."

'"What will you give me," I asked, "if I do not bury the corpse on you?"

'"Everlasting life in heaven," replied the voice.

'"How do you know this; and how am I to be sure of it?" I inquired.

'And the voice answered me, "The grave you are digging is clay. Observe now whether it will remain so, and then you will know the truth of what I tell you. And you will see that what I say will come to pass, and that you cannot bury that man on me, even if you should try to do so."

'These words were scarce ended, when the grave was turned into a mass of white sand before my face. And when I saw this, I brought the body away, and buried it elsewhere.

'It happened, some time after, that I got a new curragh made, with the hides painted red all over; and I went to sea in it. As I sailed by the shores and islands, I was so pleased with the view of the land and sea from my curragh that I resolved to live altogether in it for some time; and I brought on board all my treasures— silver cups, gold bracelets, and ornamented drinking-horns, and everything else, from the largest to the smallest article.

'I enjoyed myself for a time, while the air was clear and the sea calm and smooth. But one day, the winds suddenly arose and a storm burst upon me, which carried me out to sea, so that I quite lost sight of land, and I knew not in what direction the curragh was drifting. After a time, the wind abated to a gentle gale, the sea became smooth, and the curragh sailed on as before, with a quiet, pleasant movement.

'But suddenly, though the breeze continued to blow, I thought I could perceive that the curragh ceased moving, and, standing up to find out the cause, I saw with great surprise an old man not far off, sitting on the crest of a wave.

'He spoke to me; and, as soon as I heard his voice, I knew it at once, but I could not at the moment call to mind where I had heard it before. And I became greatly troubled, and began to tremble, I knew not why.

'"Whither art thou going?" he asked.

'"I know not," I replied; "but this I know, I am pleased with the smooth, gentle motion of my curragh over the waves."

'"You would not be pleased," replied the old man, "if you could see the troops that are at this moment around you."

'"What troops do you speak of?" I asked. And he answered:

'"All the space round about you, as far as your view reaches over the sea, and upwards to the clouds, is one great towering máss of demons, on account of your avarice, your thefts, your pride, and your other crimes and vices."

'He then asked, "Do you know why your curragh has stopped?"

'I answered, "No" and he said, "It has been stopped by me; and it will never move from that spot till you promise me to do what I shall ask of you."

'I replied that perhaps it was not in my power to grant his demand.

'"It is in your power," he answered; "and if you refuse me, the torments of hell shall be your doom."

'He then came close to the curragh, and, laying his hands on me, he made me swear to do what he demanded.

'"What I ask is this," said he; "that you throw into the sea this moment all the ill-gotten treasures you have in the curragh."

'This grieved me very much, and I replied, "It is a pity that all these costly things should be lost."

'To which he answered, "They will not go to loss; a person will be sent to take charge of them. Now do as I say."

'So, greatly against my wishes, I threw all the beautiful precious articles overboard, keeping only a small wooden cup to drink from.

'"You will now continue your voyage," he said; "and the first solid ground your curragh reaches, there you are to stay."

'He then gave me seven cakes and a cup of watery whey as food for my voyage; after which the curragh moved on, and I soon lost sight of him. And now I all at once recollected that the old man's voice was the same as the voice that I had heard come from the ground, when I was about to dig the grave for the body of the rustic. I was so astonished and troubled at this discovery, and so disturbed at the loss of all my wealth, that I threw aside my oars, and gave myself up altogether to the winds and currents, not caring whither I went; and for a long time I was tossed about on the waves, I knew not in what direction.

'At last it seemed to me that my curragh ceased to move; but I was not sure about it, for I could see no sign of land. Mindful, however, of what the old man had told me, that I was to stay wherever my curragh stopped, I looked round more carefully; and at last I saw, very near me, a small rock level with the surface, over which the waves were gently laughing and tumbling. I stepped on to the rock; and the moment I did so, the waves seemed to spring back, and the rock rose high over the level of the water; while the curragh drifted by and quickly disappeared, so that I never saw it after. This rock has been my abode from that time to the present day.

'For the first seven years, I lived on the seven cakes and the cup of whey given me by the man who had sent me to the rock. At the end of that time the cakes were all gone; and for three days I fasted, with nothing but the whey to wet my mouth. Late in the evening of the third day, an otter brought me a salmon out of the sea; but though I suffered much from hunger, I could not bring myself to eat the fish raw, and it was washed back again into the waves.

'I remained without food for three days longer; and in the afternoon of the third day, the otter returned with the salmon. And I saw another otter bring firewood; and when he had piled it up on the rock, he blew it with his breath till it took fire and lighted up. And then I broiled the salmon and ate till I had satisfied my hunger.

'The otter continued to bring me a salmon every day, and in this manner I lived for seven years longer. The rock also grew larger and larger daily, till it became the size you now see it. At the end of seven years, the otter ceased to bring me my salmon, and I fasted for three days. But at the end of the third day, I was sent half a cake of fine wheaten flour and a slice of fish; and on the same day my cup of watery whey fell into the sea, and a cup of the same size, filled with good ale, was placed on the rock for me.

'And so I have lived, praying and doing penance for my sins to this hour. Each day my drinking-vessel is filled with ale, and I am sent half a wheat-flour cake and a slice of fish; and neither rain nor wind, nor heat, nor cold, is allowed to molest me on this rock.'

This was the end of the old man's history. In the evening of that day, each man of the crew received the same quantity of food that was sent to the old hermit himself, namely, half a cake and a slice of fish; and they found in the vessel as much good ale as served them all.

The next morning he said to them, 'You shall all reach your own country in safety. And you, Maildun, you shall find in an island on your way, the very man that slew your father; but you are neither to kill him nor take revenge on him in any way. As God has delivered you from the many dangers you have passed through, though you were very guilty, and well deserved death at His hands; so you forgive your enemy the crime he committed against you.'

After this they took leave of the old man and sailed away.

Soon after they saw a beautiful verdant island, with herds of oxen, cows, and sheep browsing all over its hills and valleys; but no houses nor inhabitants were to be seen. And they rested for some time on this island, and ate the flesh of the cows and sheep.

One day, while they were standing on a hill, a large falcon flew by; and two of the crew, who happened to look closely at him, cried out, in the hearing of Maildun:

'See that falcon! he is surely like the falcons of Erin!'

'Watch him closely,' cried Maildun; 'and observe exactly in what direction he is flying!'

And they saw that he flew to the south-east, without turning or wavering.

They went on board at once; and, having unmoored, they sailed to the south-east after the falcon. After rowing the whole day, they sighted land in the dusk of the evening, which seemed to them like the land of Erin.

On a near approach, they found it was a small island; and now they recognised it as the very same island they had seen in the beginning of their voyage, in which they had heard the man in the great house boast that he had slain Maildun's father, and from which the storm had driven them out into the great ocean.

They turned the prow of their vessel to the shore, landed, and went towards the house. It happened that at this very time the people of the house were seated at their evening meal; and Maildun and his companions, as they stood outside, heard a part of their conversation.

Said one to another, 'It would not be well for us if we were now to see Maildun.'

'As to Maildun,' answered another, 'it is very well known that he was drowned long ago in the great ocean.'

'Do not be sure,' observed a third; 'perchance he is the very man that may waken you up some morning from your sleep.'

'Supposing he came now,' asks another, 'what should we do?'

The head of the house now spoke in reply to the last question; and Maildun at once knew his voice:

'I can easily answer that,' said he. 'Maildun has been for a long time suffering great afflictions and hardships; and if he were to come now, though we were enemies once, I should certainly give him a welcome and a kind reception.'

When Maildun heard this he knocked at the door, and the doorkeeper asked who was there; to which Maildun made answer.

'It is I, Maildun, returned safely from all my wanderings.'

The chief of the house then ordered the door to be opened; and he went to meet Maildun, and brought himself and his companions into the house. They were joyfully welcomed by the whole household; new garments were given to them; and they feasted and rested, till they forgot their weariness and their hardships.

They related all the wonders God had revealed to them in the course of their voyage, according to the word of the sage who says, 'It will be a source of pleasure to remember these things at a future time.'

After they had remained here for some days, Maildun returned to his own country. And Diuran Lekerd took the five half-ounces of silver he had cut down from the great net at the Silver Pillar, and laid it, according to his promise, on the high altar of Armagh.

THE HERO OF MICHAN

James Joyce

In Inisfail the fair there lies a land, the land of holy Michan. There rises a watchtower beheld of men afar.There sleep the mighty dead as in life they slept, warriors and princes of high renown. A pleasant land it is in sooth of murmuring waters, fishful streams where sport the gunnard, the plaice, the roach, the halibut, the gibbed haddock, the grilse, the dab, the brill, the flounder, the mixed coarse fish generally and other denizens of the aqueous kingdom too numerous to be enumerated. In the mild breezes of the west and of the east the lofty trees wave in different directions their first class foliage, the wafty sycamore, the Lebanonian cedar, the exalted planetree, the eugenic eucalyptus and other ornaments of the arboreal world with which that region is thoroughly well supplied. Lovely maidens sit in close proximity to the roots of the lovely trees singing the most lovely songs while they play with all kinds of lovely objects as for example golden ingots, silvery fishes, crans of herrings, drafts of eels, codlings, creels of fingerlings, purple seagems and playful insects. And heroes voyage from afar to woo them, from Elbana to Slievemargy, the peerless princes of unfettered Munster and of Connacht the just and of smooth sleek Leinster and of Cruachan's land and of Armagh the splendid and of the noble district of Boyle, princes, the sons of kings.

And there rises a shining palace whose crystal glittering roof is seen by mariners who traverse the extensive sea in barks built expressly for that purpose and thither come all herds and fatlings and first fruits of that land for O'Connell Fitzsimon takes toll of them, a chieftain descended from chieftains. Thither the extremely large wains bring foison of the fields, flaskets of cauliflowers, floats of spinach, pineapple chunks, Rangoon beans, strikes of tomatoes, drums of figs, drills of Swedes, spherical potatoes and tallies of iridescent kale, York and Savoy, and trays of onions, pearls of the earth, and punnets of mushrooms and custard marrows and fat vetches and bere and rape and red green yellow brown russet sweet big bitter ripe pomellated apples and chips of strawberries and sieves of gooseberries, pulpy and pelurious, and strawberries fit for princes and raspberries from their canes.

I dare him, says he, and I doubledare him. Come out here, Geraghty, you notorious bloody hill and dale robber!

And by that way wend the herds innumerable of bell-wethers

and flushed ewes and shearling rams and lambs and stubble geese and medium steers and roaring mares and polled calves and long-wools and storesheep and Cuffe's prime springers and culls and sowpigs and baconhogs and the various different varieties of highly distinguished swine and Angus heifers and polly bullocks of immaculate pedigree together with prime premiated milchcows and beeves: and there is ever heard a trampling, cackling, roaring, lowing, bleating, bellowing, rumbling, grunting, champing, chew-ing, of sheep and pigs and heavyhooved kine from pasturelands of Lush and Rush and Carrickmines and from the streamy vales of Thomond, from M'Gillicuddy's reeks the inaccessible and lordly Shannon the unfathomable, and from the gentle declivities of the place of the race of Kiar, their udders distended with superabun-dance of milk and butts of butter and rennets of cheese and farmer's firkins and targets of lamb and crannocks of corn and oblong eggs, in great hundreds, various in size, the agate with the dun.

The figure seated on a large boulder at the foot of a round tower was that of a broadshouldered deepchested stronglimbed frank-eyed redhaired freely freckled shaggybearded widemouthed largenosed longheaded deepvoiced barekneed brawnyhanded hairylegged ruddyfaced, sinewyarmed hero. From shoulder to shoulder he measured several ells and his rocklike mountainous knees were covered, as was likewise the rest of his body wherever visible, with a strong growth of tawny prickly hair in hue and toughness similar to the mountain gorse (*Ulex Europeus*). The widewinged nostrils, from which bristles of the same tawny hue projected, were of such capaciousness that within their cavernous obscurity the fieldlark might easily have lodged her nest. The eyes in which a tear and a smile strove ever for the mastery were of the dimensions of a goodsized cauliflower. A powerful current of warm breath issued at regular intervals from the profound cavity of his mouth while in rhythmic resonance the loud strong hale reverberations of his formidable heart thundered rumblingly causing the ground, the summit of the lofty tower and the still loftier walls of the cave to vibrate and tremble.

He wore a long unsleeved garment of recently flayed oxhide reaching to the knees in a loose kilt and this was bound about his middle by a girdle of plaited straw and rushes. Beneath this he wore trews of deerskin, roughly stitched with gut. His nether extremities were encased in high Balbriggan buskins dyed in lichen purple, the feet being shod with brogues of salted cowhide laced with the windpipe of the same beast. From his girdle hung a row of seastones which dangled at every movement of his portentous frame and on these were graven with rude yet striking art the tribal images of many Irish heroes and heroines of antiquity, Cuchulin, Conn of hundred battles, Niall of nine hostages, Brian of Kincora, the Ardri Malachi, Art MacMurragh, Shane O'Neill, Father John Murphy, Owen Roe, Patrick Sarsfield, Red Hugh O'Donnell, Red Jim MacDermott, Soggarth Eoghan O'Growney, Michael Dwyer, Francy Higgins, Henry Joy M'Cracken, Goliath, Horace Wheatley, Thomas Conneff, Peg Woffington, the Village Blacksmith, Captain Moonlight, Captain Boycott, Dante Alighieri, Christopher Columbus, S. Fursa, S. Brendan, Marshal MacMahon, Charlemagne, Theobald Wolfe Tone, the Mother of the Maccabees, the Last of the Mohicans, the Rose of Castille, the Man for Galway, The Man that Broke the Bank at Monte Carlo, The Man in the Gap, The Woman Who Didn't, Benjamin Franklin, Napoleon Bonaparte, John L. Sullivan, Cleopatra, Savourneen Deelish, Julius Caesar, Paracelsus, sir Thomas Lipton, William Tell, Michelangelo, Hayes, Muhammad, the Bride of Lammermoor, Peter the Hermit, Peter the Packer, Dark Rosaleen, Patrick W. Shakespeare, Brian Confucius, Murtagh Gutenberg, Patricio Velasquez, Captain Nemo, Tristan and Isolde, the first Prince of Wales, Thomas Cook and Son, the Bold Soldier Boy, Arrah na Pogue, Dick Turpin, Ludwig Beethoven, the Colleen Bawn, Waddler Healy, Angus the Culdee, Dolly Mount, Sidney Parade, Ben Howth, Valentine Greatrakes, Adam and Eve, Arthur Wellesley, Boss Croker, Herodotus, Jack the Giantkiller, Gautama Buddha, Lady Godiva, The Lily of Killarney, Balor of the Evil Eye, the Queen of Sheba, Acky Nagle, Joe Nagle, Alessandro Volta, Jeremiah O'Donovan Rossa, Don Philip O'Sullivan Beare. A couched spear of acuminated granite rested by him while at his feet reposed a savage animal of the canine tribe whose stertorous gasps announced that he was sunk in uneasy slumber, a supposition confirmed by hoarse growls and spasmodic movements which his master repressed from time to time by tranquillising blows of a mighty cudgel rudely fashioned out of paleolithic stone.

Who comes through Michan's land, bedight in sable armour? O'Bloom, the son of Rory: it is he. Impervious to fear is Rory's son: he of the prudent soul.

THE RETURN OF CUCHULAIN

Eimar O'Duffy

*　*　*

The Philosopher came upon the spirits of the heroes walking in the meadows of asphodel in Tir na nOg. They were not like the spirit of Socrates, which resembled a still flame; but they had the forms of men, glorious and ethereal. A hero is a person of superabundant vitality and predominant will, with no sense of responsibility or humour, which makes him a nuisance on earth; but he is in his element in the third heaven. There the heroes take themselves and one another at their own valuation, regarding their weaknesses as strength, their defects as merits. Their life is in their fame: every time an earthly orator recites their names they experience thrills of pleasure; if they are forgotten they die.

The Philosopher recognised many of the heroes as they walked in golden sunlight over the meadows of asphodel: Hector and Achilles arm in arm; Horatius in friendly colloquy with the Tusculan Mamilius; Henry V. of England; Patrick Sarsfield and Shane O'Neill; Bertrand du Guesclin; Garibaldi; and there were many more whom he did not know, mighty men of every race and nation that has shed blood on the green fields of earth. To none of these did the Philosopher address himself, but ever kept a watch for the one that seemed to him best suited for his purpose: namely, Cuchulain of Muirthemne, son of Dechtire and of Lugh of the Long Hand, of whom it was said in his time that there was none to compare with him for valour and truth, for magnanimity and courtesy, for strength and comeliness among the heroes of the world. In the crowd that went by there was none that resembled him. The Philosopher therefore passed on, and crossing another field he came to a glade, and saw before him a bush spangled with blossoms of ever-changing colours, that played sweet music in the breath of the wind. In the shadow of the bush reposed a youth of exceeding beauty. Three colours were in his hair: brown at the skin, blood-red in the middle, golden at the ends. Snow-white was his skin; as seven jewels was the brightness of his kingly eyes. Seven fingers had he on each hand; seven toes on each foot; and if you doubt it, go straightway and poke your misbelieving nose into the pages of the Book of Leinster or the Book of the Dun

Cow or the Yellow Book of Leccan, where all these things are faithfully recorded, with a good deal more that I spare you. Certain it is that it was by these marks that the Philosopher knew that the youth in front of him was Cuchulain.

By the hero's side lay a woman, with her head resting amorously on his shoulder. Very fair she was, with two plaits of hair of the rich hue of marigolds, eyes as blue as the wood anemone, and her naked body as white as the foam of the sea. The Philosopher took her at first to be Emer; but presently in their love talk, which held him entranced as by celestial music, he heard Cuchulain call her Fand; at which the Philosopher was moved to indignant speech. Said he:

'I thought that affair was over since Manannan Mac Lir shook his cloak of forgetfulness between you. And surely it were only just to render to Emer in heaven that faithfulness you denied to her on earth.'

'You forget,' said Cuchulain, 'that in heaven there is no marrying nor giving in marriage. As for this'—looking down at the woman—'I am tired of it,' whereupon he cast her from him, and she vanished. 'She was but the figment of my imagination,' said he, 'made with a wish; unmade with another: for heaven is but the fulfilment of the heart's desire.'

'I do not care for this heaven,' said the Philosopher.

'Your desire is nobler,' said Cuchulain. 'You should seek a higher heaven.'

'I am not a spirit,' said the Philosopher. 'I am the mind of a man, and I have come all the way from Earth to find you.'

'What is your errand?' asked Cuchulain.

'Man,' said the Philosopher, 'is full of wickedness and folly.'

'True,' said Cuchulain. 'Tell me what wickedness and folly he has done since I left the earth.'

'In the first place,' said the Philosopher, 'he is never done fighting and killing.'

'That,' said Cuchulain, 'is foolish, but it is not wicked. I fought and killed many in my time on earth. I am since convinced of folly, but I am clear of guilt.'

'In those days,' said the mind of the Philosopher, 'men fought with men in hot blood, hand to hand, strength against strength, feat against feat, and knowing well what it was they were fighting for. But for many centuries they have been possessed of a devilish powder which enables them to kill at a distance; and by labouring hard at its improvement they have learnt how to kill without seeing one another at all. So that now when countries are at war they do not send forth armies, but each hurls millions of missiles over mountains and seas at the other, destroying lands and cities, men, women, and children, until one or other is utterly overwhelmed. Some of these missiles are so cunningly devised that when they hit they divide up into thousands of particles which riddle and macerate the body; others contain deadly poisons; others scatter the contagion of leprosy and such foul diseases through the air; others on bursting are converted into a fine dust which is borne on the wind and blinds every eye in which it finds lodgement. They inflict on each other besides a thousand more abominations of which I cannot tell you, for already I grow weaker and must soon yield to the earthward pull of my body. But you must know this also, that nobody ever knows the real cause or meaning of these wars, and that if any one asks he is immediately put to silence.'

Said the spirit of Cuchulain: 'This is indeed a most iniquitous way of fighting. But is the tale of man's wickedness and folly complete?'

'No,' said the Philosopher. 'That is only the beginning. While the many are thus fighting, the few are contriving against their liberties, and robbing them of their bread and their homes, so that all the wealth of the world has now passed into the hands of usurers. And at last, infamy of infamies, these have begun to covet the beauty of the world as well.' Then he told Cuchulain of the bird-purchase of King Goshawk; and at that the hero was thrown into a rage surpassing even that of Socrates.

'Enough!' said he. 'I will rest here no longer. Let us to earth at once.'

*　　*　　*

So the Philosopher's mind returned to him in the little room in the back lane off Stoneybatter; and having rubbed his natural eyes he saw the spirit of Cuchulain standing before him, glorious and resplendent as a flame in a dark place, as a fountain among stagnant waters.

'Welcome to Earth and to my humble abode,' said the Philosopher. 'And pray pardon me if I leave you for a moment: for I must find you a body, in order that you may go inconspicuously among men, and see for yourself the folly and wickedness from which you would redeem them.' And at that he took himself off, leaving the hero gazing in bewilderment at the strange habitation of the heir of the ages.

Now there was a man dwelling on the same floor as the Philosopher who thought life was not worth living; for he had to spend most of it making up pounds and half-pounds of tea, sugar, flour, butter, cheese, bacon, sausages, and the like into parcels, and being polite to the fools that bought them; and he had to subsist himself on the same commodities, which he hated with the same intensity and for the same reason as the slaves who built the Pyramids must have hated the architecture of Ancient Egypt. He felt that it was no life for a man to rise in the morning before the sun had taken the chill from the air, to be at every one's beck and call during the best hours of the day, and not to be free till its tag end when there was nothing to do but sit in a stuffy picturehouse puffing fags. Of course there were also Saturday afternoons and Sundays: but what could you do with a half-day beyond killing time at the pictures or a football match? and most of a Sunday was gone by the time you had heard Mass and finished dinner, and the picture-houses didn't open till eight o'clock. Oh, it was a hard life and a dull life to be doomed to, very different from the life of his dreams. He would have liked to be rich, to be exquisitely dressed, to live in a gorgeous house, to have abundance of leisure, to have silent, smoothlygliding servants and automobiles always at his command, to be loved and won by glorious shining women— in short, to live like the heroes of his favourite film dramas. Instead of that he had to work, to obey orders, to loiter aimlessly between whiles, to wear cheap ready-made suits, to dodge other people's motors and serve their servants with sugar and sausages, and every hour of the day to be tempted by the sight of women customers and passers-by with pretty ankles and swelling hips and bosoms, that would stir up hot tormenting passions which he could only satisfy by risking damnation to eternal brimstone, or else by getting married—which he couldn't afford, and besides the girl he was walking out with was no great marvel, with her pale lips and her flat chest and her thin legs that didn't properly fill her stockings. Oh, a very dull life, thought Mr Robert Emmett Aloysius O'Kennedy.

It was to this man that the Philosopher came seeking the loan of a body. He was standing before his mirror wondering whether he ought to wash his neck that morning when he heard the Philosopher's knock.

'Come in and sit down,' he said hospitably, for he liked the Philosopher, thinking him an amusing old ass. 'You don't mind if I go on washing?' he added. 'Because I'll be late if I don't,' and, having decided to spare his neck for yet another day, he began vigorously to sponge his face.

'You told me the other day,' said the Philosopher, 'that you didn't consider life worth living.'

'I did,' said Mr O'Kennedy.

'Do you still think the same?' asked the Philosopher.

'I do,' said Mr O'Kennedy, and began to dry his face in an exceedingly dirty towel.

'Would you like to quit it for a time?' asked the Philosopher.

'I'd like to quit it for good,' said Mr O'Kennedy emphatically.

'For ever is a long time,' said the Philosopher. 'But I think we could manage a month.'

Mr O'Kennedy would have winked here if there had been anybody to wink at. The old boy was certainly more cracked than usual this morning.

'What is your body worth?' asked the Philosopher.

'Couldn't be sure,' said Mr O'Kennedy. 'The boss pays me three quid a week for the use of it, but I think he includes my soul in the bargain.'

'Your body is all I want,' said the Philosopher. 'What do you say to two pounds ten? And while I'm using it your soul can go off to heaven for a rest.'

'Done,' said Mr O'Kennedy, who thought he had a yarn that would keep his friends in stitches for a week.

Then the Philosopher put Mr O'Kennedy sitting in a chair; and he made three passes with his hands; at which the body of the young man became fixed and immovable, and his soul was filled with fear.

'Stop!' he cried. 'You are killing me.'

'You said that was what you wanted,' said the Philosopher.

'I didn't mean it,' said Mr O'Kennedy.

Then the Philosopher made three more passes; and the soul of the young man departed from him, and went wandering into space.

But the Philosopher took his body, and stripped it, and washed it thoroughly, and brought it to his own room, where he set it down before Cuchulain, saying:

'Come, now. Here is a body: a poor thing; a pitiful thing; not too well made, and somewhat marred in use; but still a semblable human body. Put it on.'

Cuchulain looked at the body and did not like it at all; for it was meanly shaped, without sign of beauty or strength. The muscles were small and flabby; the spine curved; the feet distorted fantastically by ill-fitting boots: a body unsuited to a hero. Cuchulain picked it up distastefully, as one might handle another's soiled combinations. Then he gave it a shake and clasped it to him; the spirit seemed to melt and blend with the body; and presently the heart of Robert Emmett Aloysius O'Kennedy began to beat, his lungs to breathe, his eyes to open, and his limbs to stretch themselves, as if the soul within were testing its new tenement. For some minutes after the figure stood motionless, with introspective eyes, like one in contemplation. Then came a lightning change: convulsions seized upon the body of Mr O'Kennedy, and in an instant Cuchulain had cast it from him with a cry of horror.

'O pitiful brain of man,' he said. 'What fears, what habits, what ordinances, what prohibitions have stamped you slave. I thought just now that I was in a very sweat of terror of some dreadful being named the Boss, who held over me mysterious powers, and from whom I anticipated chastisement if I were late in his service today, as I most assuredly expected to be. At the same time I felt a certain small satisfaction in remembering that yesterday I had done him some underhand injury which he would be unable to trace to my account. It was but a small weed of joy in a forest of fears. I had a fear that a man I knew might have heard that I had spoken ill of him that day; and another fear that a man I had lied to might find me out. I had also a fear that my clothes were not quite the same as were worn by every one else, and a fear of what all the people I knew might be saying or thinking of me at the moment. Then there was in me a fear that had been inspired some time ago by a play I had seen, which made me seem to myself a mean, stupid, and malicious creature; and of that fear there was born in me a hatred of the play and of the man who wrote it. I hated him for using the theatre, where I went to enjoy myself, as a means of making me hate myself. And that recalled to my memory the worst fear of all those that beset me. For in the same theatre a few days before I had watched some women dancing, and my eyes had feasted on the roundness of their limbs, and my body had been bathed in warm desires. For that sin I was damned eternally to a pit of flame unless I should repent and confess. I was afraid to confess, for fear of what the druid should think of me: and I was afraid not to confess for fear of the pit of flame. Then I began to make excuses for myself, saying that I had not looked very long and that after all there had not been much to see, so that I had not sinned mortally, and had earned only some temporary fire. But I could not make myself feel quite sure of that; nor could I decide whether I was more afraid of the confession or the pit of fire. Then I began to wonder whether there was really a God or a pit of fire at all. But I dared not let myself think of that, lest I should be struck dead and buried in the pit of fire forthwith: whereupon I—even I, Cuchulain—was seized with a loathsome terror, to escape which I cast the foul body from me. And let you, O Philosopher, remove it now; for I swear by the sunlight of Tir na nOg that I will not take to me such a horror again.'

'That is not spoken like Cuchulain,' replied the Philosopher, 'who in the olden times, when he was a man and a hero, was never known to look back from a task that he had once undertaken. It is clear, however, that the spirit is affected by the condition of the somatic substrate on which it depends for expression, so I will clean it up and let you try it on again.'

So saying the Philosopher took scalpel and forceps, and, having opened the skull of Robert Emmett Aloysius O'Kennedy, and carefully reflected the membranes, he exposed the brain to the full glare of the morning sun. Then in a bottle he compounded a lotion of carbolic acid, cold horse sense, and common soap, with which he thoroughly scoured and irrigated both the psychical centres of the cerebral cortex and the association fibres connecting them with each other and with the sensory centres: for, as Halliburton or another hath it, *Nihil est in intellectu quod non prius in sensu fuerit.* After this operation, Cuchulain entered again into the body, which straightway began to glow with a divine beauty. The skin glistened like white satin; great muscles swelled and rippled beneath it; the chest expanded to a third as much again as it was; the back straightened like a spring released; the eyes flashed fire; and the sheepish countenance of Robert Emmett Aloysius O'Kennedy shone like that of a hero in his feats. Again Cuchulain began to test the strength of his borrowed frame, stretching the arms above his head, expanding the chest, stamping the feet on the ground: until at last the Philosopher cried:

'Hold now! Enough! Do you not remember all the war-chariots and the swords and spears you broke in the testing the day you first took arms and went foraying against the Dun of Nechtan's sons? This bag of bones is too frail for such experimenting, and if you wreck it I cannot get you another. Besides it is only hired by the week.'

Then sounded the voice of Cuchulain from the vocal chords of Robert Emmett Aloysius O'Kennedy like a symphony of Beethoven from the brass trumpet of a cheap gramophone, saying: 'Excellent advice, O Sage, and none too soon, for already I feel my shoulders crack. I will forbear in other respects, but the ghosts of my seven toes are most uncomfortably crammed into the warped and etiolated extremities of this starveling here, so that I seem to tread on dried peas: therefore stretch them I must.' So he sat down, and began bunching his toes as one might do to expand a shrunken stocking; and with the effort the metatarsal bones straightened out, the phalanges uncurled, a shower of corns and bunions fell on the floor, and the two feet, which had hitherto looked more like the bleached rhizomes of some unknown plant than any part of an intelligent animal, assumed a healthy shape and hue, and heroic proportions. Even so Cuchulain was not yet comfortable in his corporeal tenement, but presently said to the Philosopher, very wry in the face: 'I fear I can never wed myself peaceably to this flesh. Lo, I have here'—pointing to his belly—'a most woeful and disturbing sensation, as of a griping emptiness, and unless it is soon relieved I will abandon this carnal vesture yet again and return to Tir na nOg.'

'That is most unfortunate,' said the Philosopher. 'I had hoped you would be free of the human frailties and the physical needs which hamper us. This pain you feel is called hunger, and it is the prick of the goad with which King Flesh reminds us that we are his slaves, forcing us to cram ourselves with bread and meat, which we metabolise into energy, which we must use to procure more bread and meat, thus remaining in a vicious circle of uselessness, eating to live and living to eat, instead of turning our minds to the

130

pursuit of wisdom. And now that I come to think of it, I am hungry myself, and no wonder, for I have forgotten how long it is since my last meal. Have patience now, and in a moment both our pangs shall be assuaged.'

The Philosopher then went out, and in a shop at the corner of the street he bought a loaf of bread, a piece of cheese, and a quart of milk; on which provender he and Cuchulain fared right joyously, charging their batteries with peptone and the other approved albuminoids, not forgetting a due proportion of vitamins as prescribed by the medical columns of the Sunday papers. Believe me, bread and cheese and milk is the best food in the world for hungry men, when you can trust your dairyman and beer is under a ban: the proof of which is that when Cuchulain had finished he rose from his chair, and, stretching himself, put a foot through the floor and both hands through the ceiling.

'Steady!' said the Philosopher. 'This is not Bricriu's Palace. It is time your limbs were fettered with the garments of civilised society.' So saying, he took out some spare ones of his own and showed Cuchulain how to put them on. Be sure that Cuchulain in donning the trousers and tucking in the shirt showed no more grace or dignity than your mortal man—poet, priest, politician, soldier, average fool, or father of ten. I wish, indeed, that all men who hold position or notoriety could be compelled to put on their trousers publicly at least once a year: by which means we should rid ourselves of a vast quantity of that humbug and hero-worship which make the world intolerable for honest and self-reliant men. For, as the proverb says, no man is a hero to his valet: the reason being that the valet sees the hero getting into his trousers.

* * *

Thus clothed and fed, Cuchulain set forth with the Philosopher to explore the city. What a sight was here for eyes accustomed to the splendours of Tir na nOg. Come, O Muse, whoever you be, that stood by the elbow of immortal Zola, take this pen of mine and pump it full of such foul and fetid ink as shall describe it worthily. To what shall I compare it? A festering corpse, maggot-crawling, under a carrion-kissing sun? A loathly figure, yet insufficient: for your maggot thrives on corruption, and grows sleeker with the progression of putridity (O happy maggot, whom the dross of the world trammels not, had you but an immortal soul how surely would it aspire heavenward!). But your lord of creation rots with his environment; so the true symbol of our city is a carrion so pestilent that it corrupts its own maggots.

What ruin and decay were here: what filth and litter: what nauseating stenches. The houses were so crazy with age and so shaken with bombardments that there was scarce one that could stand without assistance: therefore they were held together by plates and rivets, or held apart by cross-beams, or braced up by scaffoldings, so that the street had the appearance of a dead forest. (Was it not a strange perversity that slew the living tree to lengthen the days of these tottering skeletons?) Many of the houses were roofless; others were inhabited only in their lower storeys; some had collapsed altogether, and squatters had built them huts of wood or mud or patchwork on the hard-pounded rubble. The streets were ankle-deep in dung and mire; craters yawned in their midst; piles of wrecked masonry obstructed them. Rivulets ran where the gutters had been. Foul sewer smells issued from holes and cracks.

Fit lairage was this for the tragomaschaloid mob that jostled the celestial visitor to the realms of earth. What stink of breath and body assailed his nostrils; what debased accents, raucous voices, and evil language offended his hearing; what grime, what running sores, what raw-rimmed eye-sockets, what gum-suppuration and tooth-rot, what cavernous cheeks, what leering lips and hopeless eyes, what pain-twisted faces, what sagging spines, what streeling steps, what filthy ragged raiment covering what ghastly-imagined hideousness of body sickened his beauty-nurtured sight.

Yet with all this putridity and squalor there were not wanting, even in those bygone days, many signs of progress and private enterprise. At every street corner there were loud-speakers which yelled forth news and advertisements. Airplanes circled like great dragon-flies in the sky, squirting out smoke-signals such as: 'Read Cumbersome's Papers', 'Why have a Bad Leg? Try Popham's Pills', 'Trust the Trusts that Feed You', 'Vote for Coddo', '*To him that hath shall be given.* Scripture backs the Trusts', 'Are you Languid? Try Peppo'. But these were but superficial signs of civilisation. If the hero had taken the pains to inquire, he would have learnt that every foot of land in the neighbourhood was worth fabulous sums of money; and that by a miracle of organisation every square inch of rag on the backs of the people, and every crust fermenting in their bellies had helped to make millions for somebody. Cuchulain, however, was too preoccupied with the uglier side of things to make any such inquiries. Was he not a morbid ghoul and gloomy pessimist thus to nose and grope in the dark for hidden horrors, with the best of life dancing before him in the warm sunshine?

In the pother and hurly-burly I have described, owing to the celestial vigour of Cuchulain, which was chafed rather than impaired by his catatheosis, and to the enfeeblement of the Philosopher, in whom the milk and cheese had not yet replenished the loss of tissue occasioned by his fast, the two became separated, Cuchulain pursuing his way alone, and the Philosopher, after a vain attempt to overtake him, returning to his lodging. Cuchulain, however, not perceiving the loss of his companion, strode onward with more than earthly vigour, to the grave detriment of his borrowed body, which was thereby shaken up, loosened, and derivetted, like a cheap car fitted with a too powerful engine, so that soon the stomach of Robert Emmett Aloysius O'Kennedy began to clamour for more nutriment.

Just as this clamour was beginning to be unbearable, Cuchulain espied a shop window most alluringly arrayed, with a cargo more varied and of more diverse origins than ever was carried by Venetian argosy or Corinthian trireme or galley of Tyre or ancient Sidon. There were oranges there from Jaffa and Seville, and little golden tangerines from Africa nestling in silver tinfoil. There were lemons from Italy and Spain; olives and currants from the land of Hellas; raisins from the Levant, and sultanas and muscatels. Figs were there from Smyrna, and dates from Morocco, Tripoli, and Cyrenaica; bananas, the long straight kind, from Jamaica, and short curved ones from the Canaries; and pineapples and cocoanuts from the islands whose palm-trees fan the Pacific. Then there were cheeses of a hundred species: great Stiltons like mouldy casks from a tangle of jetsam; Gorgonzola streaked like marble; rich yellow English Gloucester; Dutch cheeses like bloated beetroots; hygienic cheeses done up in jars to keep in the vitamines; evanescent-flavoured Gruyère and sharp-fanged Roquefort; simple chaste Cheddar, and sensuous Camembert. There were teas also from China, India, and Ceylon, coffee from the East

Indies, cocoa from Brazil and Ecuador, and sugar from five continents and a hundred isles. Rice was there from many lands—China and Japan, Persia and Siam; and with it were pearly sago and slippery tapioca. There were tinned sardines there from France and Scotland; tinned salmon and potted meat from America. From Canada there was shredded wheat and macaroni; and macaroni also from Italy. Great pyramids of apples there were, from England and from the home orchards: some red as the blush of a country maiden, some yellow like shining taffety; with pale Newtown pippins and quiet green baking apples. Over all hung fine well-smoked hams and bacon flitches from Denmark (with a few from Limerick), and American bacon like greasy tallow. And there were biscuits and chocolates and candied fruits and nuts and odds and ends from the Lord knows where. All these things came as tribute to the men of Eirinn: they made nothing for themselves.

Here, therefore, Cuchulain turned in that he might find the wherewithal to appease the revolt of the baser nature he had put on; but he had scarce set foot in the shop before he was accosted by a large and ferocious person with stand-up hair and waxed moustaches, who, hauling him forward by the lapel of his coat, bawled into his face: 'What's the meaning of this, you blasted young slacker? An hour late! You can leave this day week; and go behind the counter this minute and make up the orders or I'll smash your face in.'

'Sir,' said Cuchulain, 'I know not what your rank is, nor what you take me for. Howbeit, I am not used to being handled thus, or being spoken to in such fashion as you have assailed me withal. Loose me, therefore, lest the grossness of this body which I am wrapped in should foul my spirit with thoughts of anger.'

The Manager, however, had not in all his life been conscious of the image of God in any shop boy: neither were his eyes opened now. Therefore, taking a stronger hold of Cuchulain, he would have thrust him ignominiously before him, had not the hero, by a sudden exertion of his muscles, maintained himself as if rooted to the floor.

'Come on, now, you obstinate young devil!' cried the Manager, giving him a flip on the ear with his great fat hand.

Anger came on Cuchulain at that, and a terrible appearance came over him. Each hair of his head stood on end, with a drop of blood at its tip. One of his eyes started forth a hand's-breadth out of its socket, and the other was sucked down into the depths of his breast. His whole body was contorted. His ribs parted asunder, so that there was room for a man's foot between them; his calves and his buttocks came round to the front of his body. At the same time the hero-light shone around his head, and the Bocanachs and Bananachs and the Witches of the Valley raised a shout around him. For such was his appearance when his anger was upon him; as testify the Yellow Book of Leccan and the other chronicles; which, if any man doubt, let him search his conscience whether he have not believed even stranger things printed in newspapers. For myself, I think the chroniclers are the more trustworthy, as they are certainly the more entertaining; for, if they lie, they lie for the fun of it, whereas the journalists lie for pay, or through sheer inability to observe or report correctly.

Now when the Manager of MacWhatsisname's grocery saw Cuchulain facing him in the same dreadful guise wherein he overcame Ferdiad at the ford and drove Fergus before him from the field of Gairech, the strength went out of his limbs, and the corpuscles of his blood fled in disgraceful rout to seek refuge in the inmost marrow of his bones. Dreadful were the scenes that were then enacted in the arched and slippery dark purple passages of his venous system. Smitten with a common panic, Red Cells, Lymphocytes, and Phagocytes rushed in headlong confusion down the peripheral veins, which soon became choked with swarming struggling masses of fugitives. Millions of smaller Lymphocytes and Mast Cells perished in the crush, but the immense mobs poured on towards the larger vessels. Yet even here there was no relief: for as each tributary stream ingurgitated its protoplasmic horde, these too became stuffed to suffocation; so that, though every corpuscle strove onward with all his strength, the jammed and stifled cell mass could scarce be seen to move. Here and there bands of armed Phagocytes, impatient of delay, tried to cut themselves a passage through the helpless huddled mass of Lymphocytes and Platelets: but they succeeded only in walling themselves up with impenetrable mounds of slaughtered carcases. Still more frightful scenes occurred when two mobs, travelling by anastomosing vessels, met each other head to head: for while those in front fought in grim despair for possession of the road until it was totally blocked and thrombosed with their bodies, the cells behind, still harried by fear, pressed onward as vigorously as ever, to the great discomfiture of the dense crowds packed between, who, thus driven by an irresistible force against an impenetrable obstacle, perished in millions.

Thus was the Manager's blood very literally curdled. And straightway Cuchulain made his salmon-leap and fisted him a smasher under the third waistcoat button, breaking four of his ribs, and hurling him backwards against the counter with enough force to crack the front of it; yet he was so well covered behind that he took no further hurt, though by his screams you would have thought he had been dumped upon the hob of hell. Then, having wrecked the shop and all it contained, Cuchulain went forth into the street, breaking a thigh or a collar-bone for any that attempted to stop him: for all which he was most soundly rated by the Philosopher when he returned to him at the close of the day.

'What have I done?' said the Philosopher. 'Old footling dunderhead that I am. What have I fetched out of heaven to show mankind his wickedness and folly? Have you no respect for our civilisation that you must sally forth, as fiery-wild as upon that first foray of yours in the barbarous youth of the world, and the first grocer's shop you come to, must leave your sign of hand upon it as though it had been the Dun of Nechtan's sons. This will never do. If two thousand years of heaven have not tamed your soul, you must tame it now; or if it is the body of Mr O'Kennedy that is at fault, then you must bring it into subjection right rapidly: for this sort of thing cannot be done in these days.'

'What,' said Cuchulain, 'have you no such pests now as these sons of Nechtan whose Dun lay athwart the road out of Ulster into Meath, and they took toll of blood and treasure of all that came by? A right strong place it was, not to be easily taken; and the sons of Nechtan were protected by magic also, so that Foill, the eldest, could not be killed with edge of sword or point of lance; and Tuachel, the second, if he were not killed by the first thrust or the first cut, could not be killed at all; and the youngest, Fandall, was swifter in the water than a swallow in the air: yet I slew them all, and gave their Dun to the winds to howl in, and to the wild beasts of Sliabh Fuath for a lairage. Have you no such pests now?'

'A many!' said the Philosopher. 'Their duns lie across all the ways of the men of Ireland, and none may eat or drink or walk abroad without paying them toll. But they cannot be brought low by such tactics as these: for they are more cunningly fenced in, and protected by more potent magic, than ever were the sons of Nechtan. This Goshawk that I told you of is one of them: and I wish you would learn to control yourself, lest you find yourself in a gaol before you can cross swords with him. But, come now. When you had vindicated your honour by thrashing the grocer, what was your next exploit? Tell me all.'

'When I had left the grocer,' said Cuchulain, 'I walked farther up the street until I came to an eating-house, which I entered very gladly, as I was feeling the pangs of my adopted stomach more keenly than ever. Here I was received at first more courteously than in any other place in this earth of yours. The master of the house bowed low to me, gave me a chair by a table clothed with fine linen, and summoned a servant to attend to my wants. Right generous and goodly fare was then put before me, and I fed full, to the manifest enjoyment of this voracious body. Afterwards, when I had rested me a while, I sought out the master of the house that I might thank him for his hospitality: but in the midst of my speech I was interrupted by the aforesaid servitor, who thrust a piece of paper into my hand, saying, "Your bill, sir," whereat the master of the house said, "Good morning, sir; much obliged; pay at the desk." Then there came upon me a most noble rage, not this time out of the spleen of O'Kennedy, but out of my own soul; and I said: "Pay! Thou kindless, impious, inhospitable boor! What shall I pay?" for I had thought the place to be a hostelry for the free entertainment of strangers, such as they have in all the planets I have ever visited, and as they had in Eirinn in the olden time. Then said my host: "I don't know what part of the world you come from, stranger: but in this benighted country you don't get nothing for nothing." "Very well, then," I said, " I will pay. But not now, since I have not the wherewithal. Good day to you, therefore. I will return anon." So saying, I would have departed in peace, but the fellow laid hand on my shoulder, saying that he would not suffer me to go until I had paid what I owed. By my hand of valour, my word never was doubted before. Therefore I smote him, yet not very hard: only so as to lay him senseless at my feet, but with the life still in him.' (Here the Philosopher groaned.) 'After that,' said Cuchulain, 'two warriors, twins, clad both alike in blue, and their helmets embossed with shining steel, came to his assistance. To these I would willingly have explained the justice of the case, but before I could speak they seized upon me, so that I was compelled to defend myself. Yet, pitying their ignorance, I did them no injury, only binding them back to back with their own harness.'

The Philosopher groaned again, and said: 'How many people altogether have you maimed and killed? Speak out. Let me know the worst at once.'

'Venerable sir,' said Cuchulain, 'I maimed no more; neither did I kill any. After that I went to a picture-house, but seeing that there was a charge for admission, I did not enter. And by my hand of valour, there is no other planet in the universe—not even among the savage seventy that revolve around the Dog Star—that acts so scurvily: for pictures were meant to elevate the soul, and therefore cannot be priced.'

'What a pity you had no money,' said the Philosopher.

'After that,' said Cuchulain, 'I entered a car driven by electricity. What do you call them?' 'Trams.' 'Trams. I thank you. Your trams are tolerable. Nay, I have seen worse, but I have forgotten where. In this tram there were seventeen people, whom I observed with great interest. Nine of them wore discs of glass before their eyes, held in place by a band of metal fixed to the nose. Why did they do that?'

'To enable them to see,' said the Philosopher. 'Their eyes were bad.'

'Why?' asked Cuchulain.

'Civilisation,' said the Philosopher.

'Twelve of them,' said Cuchulain, 'had strange looking teeth of a most unnatural aspect.'

'They were false teeth,' said the Philosopher.

'What became of their own?' asked Cuchulain.

'Rotted,' said the Philosopher.

'Why?' asked Cuchulain.

'Civilisation,' said the Philosopher.

'Ten of them,' said Cuchulain, 'had complexions of a pale green colour, with dull eyes and drooping lips. What was the meaning of this?'

'They were poisoned,' said the Philosopher, 'by eating too much preserved food.'

'Why did they do that?' asked Cuchulain.

'They could afford no better.'

'Why?' asked Cuchulain.

'Civilisation,' said the Philosopher.

'Eight of them,' said Cuchulain, 'had sores on their faces; and there were two that could not sit straight, but balanced themselves tenderly on half a rump. What was wrong with them, venerable sir?'

The Philosopher, with all commendable delicacy, gave explanation of the phenomenon.

Said Cuchulain: 'The bottom of your civilisation is in no better case. Never have I seen so many and such strange diseases as upon this little planet. Yet you have learned and charitable physicians to cure these ills, whose advice was written plain upon the windows of the tram; as, for instance: *Are you jaded, weary, dispirited? Have you that tired feeling? Then try Peppo;* and, *Is your Liver bad? Mixo will set you right;* and again, *You feel well today. But who knows what loathsome diseases the Future may bring in its train? If you want to* KEEP *well, dose yourself daily with Absoluto.* How is it, then, that these diseases persist?'

'These were no physicians' prescriptions,' said the Philosopher. 'They were but the advertisements of the Patent Medicine Trust. All these sick people you saw were sick because they were poor, and so had to stint themselves in food. To pay for these pills and bottles they must stint their food again, and so again become ill.'

'I begin to understand your world,' said Cuchulain. 'While I was making these observations the Guardian of the tram came to me and held out his hand in a manner that I had at last come to know the meaning of. Can you get nothing in this world without money, my friend?'

'No,' said the Philosopher.

'Therefore,' said Cuchulain, 'I got up to leave the tram quietly, whereupon the Guardian laid hand on me as though to detain me. Nevertheless I smote him not, but, stopping, held his arm a moment, so that he paled and offered no further hindrance. Having dismounted from the tram, I accosted one who passed, asking him to direct me to Stoneybatter. Very quickly he gave me a description that I could not understand, and would have hurried away had I not detained him by the shoulder, saying: 'What, churl! is this your courtesy to a stranger? I have a mind to slay thee, but lead me on straight to Stoneybatter, and perhaps I may pardon thee.' Said the man of Dublin: 'What sort of a joker are you? Do you know who I am?' I said I did not.

'I am Solomon Beetlebrow,' quoth he, 'Minister of the Interior.' 'Your humble servant,' said I, bowing. 'But time presses, therefore lead on.' At that I took him by the ear, and in this wise he led me to Stoneybatter, but not without exciting some admiration in our course.'

THE END OF THE RAINBOW

Lord Dunsany

*   *   *

There was a conference only two days ago in my sitting-room between two gentlemen that were members of the government of this State, though I doubt if really they were anything more than the members' secretaries; and in any case we decided nothing, and I only mention it for the sake of a curious comparison, which is that the memory of the details of that conference is less vivid in my mind today than the things that I heard and saw on a morning fifty-two years ago when I drove over to see Marlin, hoping that, after all, Dr Rory may have been wrong. I went to Clonrue first, to see the doctor, impatient for some better news than what he had given me only the day before, and I even got it, for he had seen Marlin again, later that day. 'He's walking about a good deal,' he said.

'Then he'll live longer than you thought?' I asked.

'Ah, I think he will,' said the doctor.

And from that I tried to get him to say that perhaps he was wrong after all, and that Marlin would yet recover. What he said I cannot remember. But what does it matter? I was only asking him to echo my hopes. Dr Rory's words could not turn Fate back to walk the way that I wished. Yet neither he nor I ever guessed the end of Marlin.

'What way are you going?' he said to me then.

'There's only one way,' I answered.

'Ah, but you can't get down the bohereen,' he told me.

'Can't get down the bohereen?' said I.

'No,' said Dr Rory, 'they are making a road along it.'

'A road?' I exclaimed.

'Yes,' said the doctor.

'What ever for?' I asked.

'The Peat Development (Ireland) Syndicate,' he replied.

Then it was true. What had almost seemed like ravings, when Mrs Marlin told me, was mere accurate information. They were going to spoil the bog.

'But did my father ever give them leave?' I asked, clinging to a last hope, for it was not like him to allow syndicates and such things from towns to make a mess of the countryside.

'They bought an option for fifty pounds,' said the doctor. 'And now they've taken it up. You'll get a rent from them.'

'I don't want their rent,' I said. For it seemed like selling Ireland piecemeal, if they were going to cut the bog away. One did not feel like that about the turf-cutters, who all through the spring and summer had their long harvest of peat, that brought the benignant

142

influence of the bog to a hundred hearths, and that filled the air all round the little villages with the odour that hangs in no other air that I know. Indeed the very land on which the Marlins' house was standing had been once about twenty feet higher, and had been brought to that level by ages of harvests of peat, or turf as we call it. And the land that was left was still Ireland. But now it was to be cumbered with wheels and rails and machinery, and all the unnatural things that the factory was even then giving the world, as the cities began to open that terrible box of Pandora.

'Why did my father do it?' I asked.

'He only sold them the option,' said the doctor. 'He never thought they'd come here with their nonsense. And fifty pounds is fifty pounds.'

'What are they going to do?' I enquired.

'Compress the turf by machinery and sell it as coal,' he answered.

'What nonsense,' I exclaimed.

'Of course it is,' he replied. 'But there's a lot of money to be made out of a company. And when it's got an address beside a bog, and is actually working there, it will look much more real to investors than when it's only in a prospectus. Not that it doesn't catch some of them even then.'

'I wish my father hadn't done it,' I said. But that was no use.

'They'll be broke in a few years,' said the doctor.

In a few years: that seemed terribly long to a boy.

'They'll ruin the bog,' I said. 'Can no one stop them?'

'I'm afraid not,' he answered.

It seemed so wrong that all that wonderful land, so beautiful and so free, should be brought under the thraldom of business by a city so far away, that my thoughts in their desperation turned strangely to Mrs Marlin.

'Could Mrs Marlin do anything?' I asked.

'I'm afraid not,' he said.

'Couldn't she lay a curse on them?' I continued.

'She might curse their souls a bit,' said the doctor reflectively, 'but they'd think more of business.'

In despair I left him then, and went on to see Marlin.

'We'll go by the other road,' I said to Ryan. 'They're spoiling the bohereen.'

And Ryan muttered something, as though he were cursing the

Peat Development Company, but with an amateur's ill-trained curses; not like Mrs Marlin. So down the road we went, the other road from Clonrue. And, if it is not too late, why does not some museum preserve a few yards of an old road, as it used to be before even bicycles came to cover it with their thin tracks? It's clear enough in my memory, with its wandering wheel-tracks, its pale-grey stone bright in the sunlight, and the cracks that ran through it everywhere from its unstable foundation, as soon as it neared the bog; but when I and my memory are gone and all my generation, who will remember those roads? I suppose it will not matter. They will lie sleeping, deep under tarmac, those old white roads, like the stratum of a lost era for which nobody cares. But who cares aught for the past? That pin-point of light called The Present, dancing through endless night, is all that any man cares for.

So we drove down the other road, and along the side of the bog; and the little cracks were running among the wheel-tracks as though the bog had often whispered a warning, telling that he was amongst the ancient powers, of which the earthquake was one, and that he suffered roads as all these powers suffer the things of man, which is grudgingly and for a while. And half a mile or so from the Marlins' cottage, at the nearest point to which this road came to them, I got out of the trap. My walk lay over the level land from which the bog had receded, or rather from which it had been pushed back by man: on my left, all the way as I went, the cliff of the bog's edge stood like a wave of a threatening tide, dark and long and immanent. Square pools of sombre deep water lay here and there under the cliff, with a green slime floating in most of them, and the green slime teeming with tadpoles. I sat down by the brink of one of these pools and looked at it, for the sheer joy of being home again. I looked and saw little beetles navigating the dark water like bright pellets of lead, and rather seeming to be running than swimming. Then an insect with four legs skipped hurriedly over the surface, going from island to island of scarlet grass, and a skylark came by singing. Above me in the mosses beyond the top of the bog's sheer edge the curlews were nesting, their spring call ringing over the pools and the heather. Beside me a patch of peat was touched with green as though it had gone mouldy, and up from it went a little forest of buds, each on its slender stalk, for spring had come to the moss as well as the curlews. In amongst the soft moss grew what looked like large leaves, but so fungoid was their appearance that it was hard to say whether they belonged to the moss, or were even vegetable at all: rather they seemed to haunt the boundary of the vegetable kingdom as ghosts haunt the boundary of man's. Strangely ill-assorted were those gross leaves and the fairy-like slenderness of the stalks. I could have sat there long, watching the activity of the two kinds of insect that scurried over that water, or looking at the history of the ages in the coloured layers of the peat, which is always written wherever an edge of Earth is exposed, if only one can read it; and all the while the skylark sang on. I could have sat there idly all day in deep content, only that an anxiety thrilled through my content, and drove me on, urging me to hasten to hear the worst about Marlin. And so I walked on, under the bog's edge, with peaty soil underfoot, on which sometimes rushes grew, now all in flower, and sometimes heather, young and very green, and sometimes, almost timidly, the grass; for the grass came mostly along the tracks of the turf-carts, and where the earth was most trodden, and by little bridges across tiny streams, as though only in the immediate presence of man could it dare to usurp that land where the bog so recently reigned. And all the way as I went over that quiet land there went beside me a chronicle of the ancient shudders of Earth, old angers that had stirred and troubled the bog; for the long layers, tawny and sable, ochre, umber and orange, that were the ruins of long-decayed heather and bygone moss, went in waves all the way, sometimes heaving up into hills, the mark of some age-old uprising, sometimes cracked by clefts that sundered them twenty feet down, as though they still threatened the levels so lately stolen by man. And even that land that man had won for himself faintly shook as I trod it, making the threat of the bog all the more ominous. I passed innumerable little ditches, dug to run off the water that came down from the bog, so that the things of man might grow there and not the things of the wild. And over all of them were little bridges for the turf-carts to cross with their donkeys, for a man on foot could step over the ditches anywhere; trunks of small trees heaped over with peat and sods; but the trunks were all rotting away, so that only a prophet could tell whether man would hold that land, or whether the damp and the south-west wind and the bog would one day claim their own again.

Presently I came on turf-cutters at their work, digging out of the brown face of the soft cliff their foot-long sections of peat, four or five inches thick and wide, with an implement that seemed a blend between a spade and a spear. I don't suppose that has altered since I was living in Ireland, nor for some centuries before that. And another thing that can scarcely ever have altered is the little turf-cart in which the pieces of fresh wet peat are drawn away by donkeys, for it has the air of having been there for ever, and I do not see what it can ever have altered from, for it is so simply primitive that it must have been nearly the first. The superstructure was like that of the wheel-barrow and little larger, but it was the wheels that had been left behind by receding ages from man's very earliest effort at drawing loads. These were merely two trunks of trees, hollowed a little where the axles should be and leaving a pair of crude wheels at the ends. An iron bar ran through the core of each trunk, connecting it to the cart, and on these the trunks revolved. Two donkeys dragged the little load away to be stacked and to dry in the spring weather, with a little heather on top to keep off the rain. In those stacks the long, brick-like pieces of chocolate-coloured turf would dry to pale ochre and be carried to the cottages to take their part in the struggle against the next winter. Two men with long black hair were working the face of the bank as I came by, cutting in level lines, as though they were taking bricks layer by layer off a wall; so that when they had come to the blacker layers underneath, and had gone as low as they could and met the water, the edge of the bog would have receded along the width of their working a distance of four inches. We greeted each other as I passed, and I went on over grass and bare peat and rushes, and over the little bridges, till I saw far off the willows that grew near the Marlins' house, shining like sunlight coming through greenish smoke. I saw the willows that I knew so well, now glorying in the spring, but I saw with a pang light flashing on roofs that were strange to me: mean buildings had come already, with the swiftness of an encampment, to that land that had always seemed to me as enchanted as any land can be. And what would come of that enchantment now? So elusive a thing, among that cluster of huts, could never survive the noise, the ugliness, the ridicule and the greed. I felt sick at heart at the sight of them; and in my despair I knew nothing that could protect the ancient wildness that was such a rest and a solace to any cares that one brought to it from the world; and, feeling helpless myself, I placed no confidence in any help that could come from Mrs Marlin.

*   *   *

When I saw the willows shining I hurried on, for anxiety drove me on over the little bridges to hear the news of Marlin. The curlews uttered their curious cry on my left, beyond the wavy strata, while above me a skylark sang on and on and on; and, amongst all the cries of the birds and the gleam of the willows, my melancholy deepened, standing out all the blacker against the splendour of spring.

And then I saw Mrs Marlin, far off, in her garden. She was not hurrying, she was not wailing; and I knew how grief would have racked that dark woman, giving a wild movement to her strides and a certain terror to every line of her. Or if I did not know to what fury grief would have urged her spirit, I saw at least, and even at that distance, that no great passion was driving her; although later, when I came nearer, I saw often a quick uneasy turn of her head towards the new huts and the dam that was building across the stream, as though a malevolence smouldered in her, or she rested from recently cursing; but at least Marlin was not dying; and, suddenly relieved of that fear, I walked towards her with all my anxieties gone.

'How is Marlin?' I asked, when I got within call of her.

'He's all right, sir,' she said.

I came a few paces nearer.

'I am delighted to hear that,' I said to her. 'The doctor gave a very bad account of him.'

And she laughed at that, with rather a sly look.

'Ah, what does he know?' she said.

'Where is he?' I asked.

'Ah, he's gone,' she replied.

'But Marlin, I mean,' said I.

'Aye. Sure, he's gone,' she answered.

'Gone?' I said. 'Where?'

'Over the bog,' she said.

'But what way?' I asked.

'A rainbow showed him,' she said.

'A rainbow?' I muttered.

And she went to the door and opened it for me, and we went in. And she offered me a chair before her great fireplace and sat down a chair herself and gazed into the red embers of the turf, which never break into flame. And then she said: 'He was very ill. Ill as the doctor said. But, sure, what does he know of anything, only of the affairs of that world?' And she pointed away from the bog.

'He was lying there in his bed yesterday evening, ill as the doctor said, and I was trying to get him to take some medicine, when he turned to me and says: "Mother, I must go. For if I stop any longer I'll be dying. And I'll not die in this earth." And I says to him: "Ireland's a good enough land for any man to die in." And he says: "Not when it's Hell you'd have to go to; and it's where I'd go from here." And at that he rises up from his bed and puts on his boots, and gives one look round at the cottage. Then he gives me a kiss and sets off, and there was a rainbow shining. And no sooner had he climbed up by the bank of turf and set his foot on the bog, but the rainbow begins to go further and further off. And he follows it all the way to the everlasting morning.'

I don't exactly know what she meant by that, but she pointed through a window as she spoke, in the direction in which the sun usually brightened far patches of water, away by the bog's horizon, all the morning; the direction in which so often I had seen Marlin's eyes stray.

'But how far did he go?' I asked.

'To Tir-nan-Og,' she said.

'But how did he know the way?' said I.

'The rainbow showed him,' she answered.

What had happened to Marlin? I wondered. Where had he gone?

'How far did you see him?' I asked.

'Away and away,' she said. 'And the rainbow before him.'

'But he couldn't walk out of your sight,' I said. 'A sick man couldn't have done it.'

But still she pointed away to the far horizon, where the water shone and no hills bounded the bog.

'The night came on,' she said, 'after the rainbow left him.'

Her words frightened me. You can't walk the bog out there in the night; or it is very nearly impossible.

'You should have called him back,' I said.

'Call back a rainbow!' she exclaimed, with a gust of laughter.

'No, Marlin,' I explained.

'Nor him, either,' she said. 'They were both of them going away to the glory of Tir-nan-Og, the rainbow from the dark world and the coming of night, and my son from damnation. Little they know the rainbow from his few visits to these fields, little they know it that have not seen it glorying in its home, entwined with the apple-blossom of the Land of the Young; and little they know of a man till they have seen him in the splendour of his youth among the everlastingly youthful in the orchards of Tir-nan-Og.'

For a moment I feared she would try to go after him, and drown herself, thinking she could not go very far in safety, at her age, over the bog.

'You're not going, too?' I asked.

'I'll never see him there,' she said. 'God knows I'll never see him there, having stayed on Earth too long, till my feet are slow with its weeds and my soul with its cares. Though I'll say nothing harsh against Earth, for the sake of Ireland. And I have one thing more to do upon Earth yet. For I have to speak with the powers of bog and storm and night, and to learn their will with the men that are harming the heather.'

'Show me the way he went,' I said, and got up from the chair; for I felt sure that a man as sick as he was could never have walked far over the bog. And she rose and came with me out of the door and we walked to the bog's edge, I impatient to find Marlin and trying to hurry her, she without any anxieties and only concerned with her reflections, which she uttered as we went.

'It's by the blessing of God,' she said, 'that mothers never see their sons grow old; bent and wrinkled and haggard. It's the blessing of God. And they should not see them die. A few days more and Tommy would have died, there in his bed beside me; and no art of mine could have hindered it; for I have no power against the splendour of death. But he rose and walked away out of the world, where age cannot overtake him, and where death is only known from idle stories told in the orchards by those that are young for ever, for the sake of the touch of sadness that gives a savour to their immortal joy. Weakness and wrinkles and dying, they are the way of this world, and the shadow of damnation creeping nearer. But he has walked away from the world and away from the shadow.'

All the while I was trying to hurry her, picturing Marlin lying a mile away out in the bog, for I feared he could scarce have got further; and how would a sick man fare, out there all night?

'Was there any frost?' I asked her; for we still had a touch of frost sometimes at night, and she was nearer to these things than I in our large house.

But she only answered: 'Aye, the world's cold,' and gazed away before her with happy eyes as though she went to her son's wedding.

'Hurry,' I said, for she would not quicken her pace. 'Or we'll find him dead.'

'Ah, no,' she said. 'He would not wait for death. And why would he, with damnation prepared for him by those that are jealous of the land of the morning?'

I don't know whom she meant; and, God knows, these are no words of mine, but only hers still haunting my memory, where I fear they should not be, and would not be if I could banish them.

And so we came to the steep edge of the bog and she climbed agilely up, and I after her; and for a while we walked in silence over the rushes. The moss lay grey all round us, crisp as a dry sponge, while we stepped on the heather and rushes, the heather all covered with dead grey buds, the rushes a pale sandy colour. I had never walked the bog in the spring before, and was surprised at the greyness of it. But some bright mosses remained, scarlet and brilliant green; and along the edge of the bog under the hills lay a slender ribbon of gorse, and the fields flashed bright above it, so that the bog lay like a dull stone set in gold, with a row of emeralds round the golden ring. A snipe got up brown, and turned, and flashed white in turning. A curlew rose and sped away down the sky with swift beats of his long wings and loud outcry, giving the news, 'Man, Man,' to all whose peace was endangered by our approach, and a skylark shot up and sang, and stayed above us, singing. The pools that in the winter lay between the islands of heather, and that Marlin used to tell me were bottomless, were most of them grey slime now, topped with a crust that looked as if it might almost bear one. We knew the way to go; the way that I had so often seen Marlin's eyes gazing, the way that Mrs Marlin said straight out was the way to Tir-nan-Og: I could see the water flashing over there, though the grey moss was dry about us. The fear that I had had that Mrs Marlin would come to harm in the bog I had now entirely forgotten, for she stepped from tussock to tussock surely and firmly, with a stride that seemed to know the bog too well to falter even with age. We came, with the skylark still singing, to pools that were partly water and partly luxuriant moss: strange grasses leaned along them and burst into flower. More and more pools them we met, and less grey moss, and presently the wide lakes lay before us, to which Marlin had looked so often. I stood on a hummock of heather and stared ahead, then looked at Mrs Marlin. There was nothing but water and rushes and moss before us. We were as far as a sick man could have walked, apart from the danger and difficulty of all that lay ahead. If Marlin had come this way there was no hope for him.

'You are sure he went this way?' I asked, and knew that the question was hopeless even as I asked it.

Her face all lighted up, looking glad and young, and with shining eyes she gazed over the desolate water, and said: 'Aye, he went this way, this way; away from the world and the shadow cast by damnation, black as tar on the cities. Aye, he went this way.'

And then I knew that Marlin shared with the Pharaohs that strange eternity of the body that only Egypt and the Irish bog can give. Centuries hence, when we are all mouldered away, some turf-cutter will find Marlin there and will look on a face and a figure untouched by all those years, even as though the body had obeyed the dream after all.

* * *

Then I brought Mrs Marlin back from the bog, thinking she had gone far enough, and knowing that the part of it to which we had come was dangerous walking even for a young man. For these were the waters that Marlin called 'the sumach,' or some such word that I do not know how to spell, a mass of stored rains that grew heavier every year, till it flooded in under the roots of whatever growth gave a foothold, and floated the light surface of mosses and peat, till everything trembled round one as one walked: one called it the shaky bog, the most dangerous of all the kinds of bog that one walks. These waters were the source of the stream that ran past the Marlins' house; but, as more rain came with the storms than left with the stream, the whole weight of the bog was increasing.

'We must get all the men we can find, and search the bog for him,' I said, when I got her back to the safe grey moss and the heather. And at that she laughed with peals of her strange wild laughter.

'Aye, search the world for him,' she said. 'But he will not be there. And it's not the world that wants him, but Hell. And Hell will not have him either. It's the orchards of Tir-nan-Og that have him now, with the morning dripping from their branches in everlasting light, golden and slow, like honey. Aye, and the evening too, and both together; for Time that troubles us here comes not to those gleaming shores. Age, desolation and dying; that's the way of these fields; and not one wrinkle, nor sigh, nor one white hair, ever came to Tir-nan-Og.'

'We must look for him,' I said. For it was a duty to do all that one could, even if the search seemed hopeless; and I did not wish her words to turn me away from it, as I feared that they soon would.

'Aye, search for ever,' she said, 'and you'll never see him. But I shall see him often.'

'Where?' I said.

'Where would it be,' she answered, 'but about his mother's house and over the heather that he knew as a child, and on mosses by pools where he played? Where else would he go when he comes from Tir-nan-Og, and the jack-o'-lanterns come riding the storm through the darkness, and go dancing over the bog?'

'How will he come?' I asked.

'On the west wind,' she answered.

'We must search for him,' I said, sticking to my point, which it seemed harder and harder to do.

'Aye, search,' she said, and went off again into peals of her wild laughter, which rang far over the bog and frightened the curlews.

'How could he get to Tir-nan-Og?' I asked. For if there was any chance of finding him, it would have to be done quickly, and she would not see that it was serious at all. I spoke to her all the more impatiently for the fear that I soon should believe her, and do nothing at all. And one ought to do something.

'He'd go by the way of the bog till he came to the sea,' she said. 'Didn't he know the way well?'

'And then?' I asked.

'There'll be a boat there, lifting and dropping with the lap of the tide,' she said; 'and eight queens to row it; queens that have turned from Heaven, and yet slipped away from damnation. Hell has not their souls, nor the earth their dust.'

'How could he know they'd be there?' I asked her.

'How could he know?' she said. 'I told him.'

But that made things no clearer. Then she gazed away over the bog and went on talking: '"Hell would have me, mother," he said, "if I stay here." And when I saw he was bent on leaving the world, I said I'd help him; for he knew the way over the bog to the shore, but he'd never been on the sea. And I went one stormy night to the bog, when the wind was in the West and all the people of Tir-nan-Og were riding upon the storm, and by the edge of the water where they were flashing and admiring their heathen beauty, I called out to them: "Ancient People, there's a man that would share your everlasting glory; and Hell wants him, because he has turned his face to the West. How shall he go to find you?"

'And with tiny voices they answered me through the storm, voices shriller than the cry of the snipe and small as the song of the robin, they whose voices rang once from hill to hill over Ireland; and they said: "To the sea, to the sea."

'"And then?" I said, "Oh ancient and glorious people?"

'"What would you have of us?" they asked.

'And I lured them nearer, by a power I have, and said to them: "By that power, I need your help over the sea."

'And they said to me: "When will he come?"

'And I answered: "One of these days," which is the only time we know with the future, and all we ever will know, till it is dated and mapped as is should be.

'And they repeated one to another, with their small voices, "One of these days," till the message passed out of hearing. And I made my compact with them out there on the bog, swearing by turf and heather, as they swore by blossom and twilight. For a danger threatened the bog and I swore to guard it, and they swore to carry Tommy over the water and bring him to Tir-nan-Og. Eight fair girls, they said, that were queens of old in Ireland, would bring him over the water, waiting for him where the bog ran down to the shore, upon the day that I said. And Tommy would know them, apart from their beauty and apart from their crowns of gold, by the light that would be gleaming along the sides of the boat; for the boat would be made from the bark of birches growing in

Tir-nan-Og, and the twilight that shone on them in the Land of the Young would be shining upon them still. And whether it was night in the world, or whether noon or morning, the twilight of Tir-nan-Og would be shining upon that birch-bark.'

I tried to picture a boat glowing gently in twilight while it was noon all round, with the sun bright on the water; or, more wonderful still, the birch-bark iridescent in the soft light of the gloaming, while all around was night. But thinking of this only drifted me from my purpose, which was to find a number of men and search the heather for Marlin. I was in two minds; one was the mind that listened to Mrs Marlin telling of Tir-nan-Og, of which I had already learned so much from her son; the other, a more disciplined mind, told me that the bog must be searched for Marlin whether there seemed any hope of finding him there or not. The more useless this appeared the more I clung to it, lest Mrs Marlin should lure me to forget it altogether, and a duty remain undone.

'We must search for him,' I repeated.

'Aye, search,' she said indulgently, as though the search were some trivial rite that custom idly bound me to. And I think she knew from the tone of my voice that I somehow had not my heart in it. 'Would they fail me?' she went on. 'Never.'

And I saw from her far gaze westwards, and the light in her eyes, that she was thinking of those eight queens.

We came to the bog's edge, where deep fissures ran down out of sight, as though the vast weight of the bog were too much for the banks that bounded it; and from that high edge I looked over the land lying round Marlin's cottage that had always seemed so magical to me, the land over which the old willows brooded in winter and were like an enchantment in spring, and I could have wept at what I saw. And what I saw is well enough known: I need hardly describe it: a large number of small houses meanly built, and all exactly the same, denying any difference between the tastes of one man and another, nor caring anything for any man's taste, nor expressing any feeling or preference of builder or owner. It was as though men without any passions had built them all for the dead.

They were barely finished, but men were already living in some of them, and work had already started on building the dam and putting in the wheel that was to be turned by the water and which would set the machinery clanking in the ugly house they were building. The world is full of such things, little need to describe them; the only concern that this story has with them is to tell that they came down dark upon that spot to which first my memories went whenever I was far from Ireland, racing there quicker than homing pigeons, or bees going back to the hive. And not only had they spoiled the magic that lay over all that land, deep as mists in the autumn, but they were there for the purpose of cutting the bog away; not as the turf-cutters take it, with imperceptible harvests, slowly, as years go by, a few yards in each generation, but working it out as miners work out a stratum of coal.

It was to these men that I now appealed, calling out to them from the high edge of the bog and telling them that a man was lost out there in the heather. They came at once, and I soon had about thirty of them, some of them English and some the men of Clonrue. 'Begob,' said one of the latter to me, 'if you set English-men walking the bog it's soon a hundred men that we'll have to look for, and not only one.' But oddly enough it was the English-men that took charge as soon as we started off, though they got very wet over it.

'We'll find your son for you, mam,' said one of them. 'Don't you worry.'

But she looked fiercely at him and only answered: 'Do you know the way to World's End?'

'I expect we could find it, mam,' was all he said to her.

Her eyes were blazing, and then she burst into laughter. 'And you'll only be half-way to him then,' she said.

Then we all spread out to about half a mile and walked in the direction of the deep part of the bog, from which Mrs Marlin and I had just returned, and heard her laughter still ringing in mockery of the thirty men that were trying to find her son.

We went back over the grey moss, about twenty-five yards apart, the bog-cotton flowering round us, a bright patch at the tips of the rushes, the skylark high above us singing triumphantly on.

'It's got on her mind a bit,' said one of the men, as Mrs Marlin's laughter rang out behind us.

'I'm afraid it has,' I said. For I could not explain Mrs Marlin to an Englishman.

'We'll find him all right, sir,' he said.

But he only saw that the heather was not high enough to hide anyone lying there from a searcher passing within twelve yards: he did not know the deeps of an Irish bog.

'Don't step on the bright mosses,' I said.

We went on till Mrs Marlin's laughter faded from hearing, and the only wild cries we heard were the cries of the curlews.

When I came again to that waste of water and moss, where trembling waves ran through the bog from every footstep, the line of men drew in from either side to the edges of that morass, each man seeming drawn towards it without anyone saying a word; and we all looked over the water and brilliant mosses in silence. I realised then that in bringing these thirty men over the bog I had done a conventional duty in which there was no meaning whatever.

We turned round and each man took a different line to the one by which he had come, so as to cover more ground on the way back, but nobody searched any more. I knew that they were not searching, but said no word to them, for my thoughts were in Tir-nan-Og.

CROTTY SHINKWIN

A. E. Coppard

*   *   *

This was a little man I'm telling you, Crotty Shinkwin, a butcher
once, with livery eyes and a neck like a hen that was not often
shaved. He knocked out a sort of living by the coast of the cliff
and the sandy shore of Ballinarailin, a town full of Looneys,
Mooneys and Clooneys, the Mahoneys, Maloneys, the Dorans,
Horans and Morans, but if you were to ask what was their scheme
of life it could only be said they were seen gathering weeds from
the sea and stones from the shore, which is poor stuff anyway to
be passing the time of day on.

In his young youth Crotty bought cattle alive and sold it dead.
You would see him going into the kitchens with the large hack of
meat in one hand, a saw in the other, and a great coulter of a

knife in his mouth, and when he came out again you would observe there was the less meat on him to be carrying. But he was married ten years to Eva Clohesy, a hard woman, and so he was forced to give up that kind of life—it was too much altogether for a man that did not know the wishes of herself from one moment to another.

'Why,' says he to Peter Sisk, 'if you ask me what she likes, or what she wants, you have me beat. *She* could not tell you. It would take the help of God Almighty to keep up with her. Napoleon couldn't do it; he could not.'

So Mr Shinkwin took to fishing or to looking after the holy well, and little handicrafts like that, for there was nothing else to turn a hand to in that drifty place.

'Holy and sacred medallion!' says she to him then, 'and what are you about at all?'

She was glaring at him with her two cat's eyes, but a fine woman, one of the Clohesy's she was, as brisk as a Connemara cow, and two hairy arms.

'I am not well,' says he.

'What's on you?'

'And I never could be well again,' he says, 'not in this mortal world, and what's more—I will not.'

'Och! For a man that's about to be dying there's a deal of talk and porter in it yet!'

Crotty looked at her: 'The devil knows, you strap, and everyone knows I've a drowsiness in my bones and a creepiness in my stomach. I'm sick and I'm bad. It's wrecked I am.'

'O, you goat!' says she. 'You shanandering goat!'

'But . . . but I endure it,' Crotty said, 'as a man I endure it; I do not give in to it. By my soul, you can't daunt me, and I do not sink to my bed.'

She gave a great spit, like a man with a quid:

'The kingdom of heaven be yours, little or much.'

'And if I should come,' he continued, 'to my expiration, do not go for to put your hands on me and rouse me again.'

'The devil a hand,' says she. 'Let you walk out to the rocks now and catch me a couple of crabs, or by the harp of the Jews it's your corpse itself I'll be lathering with holy water this night.'

So Crotty would go perch himself on a stone to watch the half mile of surf roving in from the bay, and the nuns from the convent bathing in it. Giddy and gay they would be, bobbing up to their ribs and groaning, but they were dressed in blue sacks of night-gowns and long baggy trousers and offered no nice allurements to Mr Shinkwin's eye. If they took an orphan down to bathe with them, it should undress and dress on the stones outside the bit of a box they dried in, and though it blew hearty and crisp the child could not come into their holy boudoir.

'It would be queer and all,' thought Crotty, 'if the child was the nuns just now, and the nuns was the child!'

And here was Tarpy Ryan and his ass cart loading weed, and far out in the bay was Inniskalogue, a big hump of an island with nothing on it but grass, and smooth as a button. No one lived there, neither priest, peasant nor gentleman; nobody visited it— it had the bad name; no one owned it and nobody wanted it. If you asked a fellow about Inniskalogue he would twist his eyes, or he would shake his head and scratch it (or his haunches) until you wished you had not enquired of him. But it lay on the blue bosom of the sea, the sunbeams glistening, a fine sparkling pasturage with the gap of a cliff here and there.

One fine day Crotty and young P. J., a handsome lad, sailed over the bay in a yawl, and in about an hour they got so close to one corner of Inniskalogue that they could see the stones, but not a bird on it or any any other living sign. And P. J. cast anchor there for to do a little fishing. Down went the hook, the cables leaping and growling after it and after it until there was no more cable, and still they had not got a hold.

'By my soul, there's a power of deep water under us!' said P. J.

Just then, down comes a draught of air from a cloud and it puffed the yawl out round past the corner of the island. They went roving round to the far side with the anchor trailing, till they felt a jerk and the little boat shook.

'She's got a hold,' cried P. J.

And by the souls of the sainted martyrs, she had! The wind gave a great twist, the yawl reeled, and there was that island, hooked underneath by the anchor, tearing after them and following them.

'What is it and all!' Crotty shrieked, for his seven senses had gone black on him, and P. J. was too dazzled to loosen the sheet. They could not see the mainland for the island hid it from them, hundreds of acres it was, and it moving like a cork on the hills and hollows of the sea. They fell on their knees in the boat and prayed to God.

'Sir,' gabbled Crotty. 'We are perishing! For the love of heaven, mercy! Throw back that walking world and sweep the head off me, for my soul has no thirst for the waves of water. Jesus, Joseph, and Mary! Sir, if you please! Amen.'

Then, in the very nick of destruction, the island stopped, and the boat stayed and began to move backwards until it was rushing backwards towards the island. As they looked at it the island itself heaved up and twirled over like a great plate on a hinge until it was upside down. It turned as easy as a porpoise, casting no splash, with only showers dripping off it, but the great black half moon of it when it was up-ended, was as much as a side of the whole world falling, and threw a cold shadow across the yawl. It stayed upside down, and there the boat stayed too, anchored fast and the sail throbbing, and the sea rocking gently as a cradle now.

'We're stuck!' cried P. J., heaving on the rope. 'Crotty, we're stuck!'

'O, God alive!' Crotty said, pointing. 'Will you throw an eye on that!'

And he did so. The island was topsy-turvy now, its green hump was below and the roots of the island had come up from the ocean; they could see a neat little town sitting amid the drainings of a flood. The water was sweeping from it like sand from a barrel, but it dried on the moment. The weeds began to become grass and pretty fuchsias and long creepers to hang over the walls. Some big fishes that had got caught gasping in the hedges flipped into the fields and changed into sheep and went crying for their lambs. There was a little church with a steeple chiming—the bell had a pitiful note like the chink of two stones—and a score of cabins but no people seen.

'Will you tell me, Crotty, what is that there now?' P. J. was pointing toward the church steeple.

'What?' said Crotty.

'On the cross of the church? Do you see it?'

'I do see it.'

'It's my anchor!'

'God's fortune!' said Crotty, 'and how did it climb there at all?'

'And the rope of it stretching from us across the fields.'

It was true enough. The anchor had hooked in the cross of the church itself when it was upside down, and they had pulled it right over.

'I can't lose my anchor,' said P. J., 'it's Andy Mullen's anchor.'

'It is,' Crotty said.

They hauled on the anchor cable until the slack was dripping above the sea, and they pulled themselves right ashore against a path that ran up to the church.

'Go and get the anchor, Crotty.'

'O,' grumbled he, 'I was never that sort of climbing man, I haven't a wing to my elbows.'

P. J. went on coiling up the cables and readying the boat, and spitting in the sea, and staring at the island.

'Go and get the anchor, Crotty.'

Crotty, sitting on a thwart, gaped at the church steeple with repugnance. It was a small steeple, but still it was high and the anchor was on it like a crow's nest in a tree.

'I'm thinking,' said he, 'there's a bank of bog between this and that; a man would murder himself going there. And what's a bit of a hook? I'll take a pull on it, anyway.'

He pulled and pulled on the anchor rope until he was sore and tired.

'Go and get the anchor, Crotty,' said P. J. again.

Crotty sighed and sat down. 'A deceitful island,' he mused. 'No one knows the half of it, sleeping or waking. Am I alive, or is it dead we are? Is my head my head, or is it my rump?'

'Go and get the anchor, Crotty.'

'Ah, to hell with the anchor,' replied he.

P. J. stood up. 'I wonder,' said he, 'if there's a police barracks in this place.'

'Maybe,' Crotty said. 'Maybe there's a booking-office and a train to Dublin!'

P. J. took off his hat and flung it ashore.

'There goes my hat,' said he, 'and where it goes I must follow.'

So saying he stepped on the gunwale and leaped to a rock.

'God save all here!' he cried.

No one answered, but Crotty scrambled over and stood beside him. P. J. walked towards the little road, but Crotty kept still and called out: 'P. J.! Let you take a sniff round first!'

P. J. paused: 'Come on with you! Here's a notice on a board. Come and read it.'

Crotty went and read it out to him.

NOTICE

RATEPAYERS WHO HAVE FAILED TO PAY THEIR RATES NOW DUE
FOR SOMETIME ARE HEREBY INFORMED THAT STEPS ARE ABOUT TO
BE TAKEN IMMEDIATELY TO ENFORCE PAYMENT

(*Signed*) CROTTY SHINKWIN

'By the powers above, P. J., or the powers below, 'tis a disgrace
to my native land. I've seen the like of that notice before, barring
the name. I never thought my name was so common, I did not.
The buttons on your coat are the one buttons with mine, but your
name is not Shinkwin, and my name is not your name. Who is
this nigger-driver of a tax-man? Or am I doomed to a watery
grave, is it? Will I be collecting the rent from a few shrimps, d'ye
think?'

'Come on with you!' said P. J.

They went on, but they did not use the road going to the church;
they took a step aside on the turf that led them up a hill, good
honest turf, a little damp maybe, but thrifty and sound. Up, up
they went, and what with the steepness of it and the sun's warmth
Crotty was soon wishing they had never come that way or met
such a contrary island, or gone in a boat with such an ecclesiastical
turn of hook.

'I've a drought on me would blind a salamander.'

Looking here and looking there he saw no sign of life or laughter
till they came to the top, and there it was a high cliff they were
on, it dropping to the sea sixty or seventy or eighty fathoms down.
Behind them and below were the church, the cabins, the sheep,
the flowers; patches of field, and a wood of thorns; they could see
all over this turned-up island. And all round it was the tranquil
sea, but there was not a sight of the mainland or Ballinarailin
anywhere in the quarters of the hemisphere, nothing but the sea
only and the place they were on. They were stricken with the
surprise of that, and the fear of that, and the silence of it; the
power of the wind would not have loosened the flax from a ripe
thistle.

'Where in the world is the world?' moaned Crotty.

From the edge of the cliff they watched the blue seas move,
white gannets diving, and three porpoises rolling slowly along.
Halfway down the cliff a dead pig lay tumbled on a rock, a white
pig with a long red burst in its belly.

Crotty was timid as a sheep, but P. J. was staring like a man well on the road to heaven.

'Peace to my soul,' he murmured softly. 'This would be the grand place to live in with the woman you wanted and she loving you at all times. It is planted with sweet herbs, and the air is gentle with the kiss of their blossoms.'

'What is it? What is on you, P. J.?'

'Here, on this cliff for my holy tower and the wide sea shining, to go in strength and virtue like the fleet and careless birds. Or to walk with the burden of love till I might find her sleeping on the shore.'

'Ach!' growled Crotty, 'and she glaring at you with her two cat's eyes.'

Just then they saw the little man; he was sitting on the cliff with his legs dangling over. They walked up to him.

'The blessing of heaven on you, good man,' said P. J., 'but that's the queer place to be fishing!'

The man did not answer. He had the face of a weasel, and fingers like the claws of a crab.

'Is it deaf you are?'

The surly man took no heed of them at all, but was pulling up a long stout cord from the sea below. Over and over he coiled the white cord, a mighty stretch of it, until it dripped with sea, and there at the end of it was hooked a fish. The man gave its head a clout and cast it into a creel by his side. As soon as he had stuck a mussel on the hook he threw down the cord again and sat still as a stone. Presently he looked round, but he said nothing. It was as if he did not see them, although they were standing so close they could notice a flea was feeding on his ear.

'Is it blind you are?'

And Crotty bent down to tap him on the shoulder, but when he did that his two fingers sunk into nothing, as if the man was but a vapour.

'Jesus, Joseph and Mary!' yelled Crotty. 'Let me out of this!' And he ran off so fast you could not see his two feet moving at all. When he came to the boat again P. J. was beside him, laughing:

'Wait, Crotty! D'ye hear that, you stag!'

Crotty heard the church bell clinking faintly.

'There's the little anchor to fetch,' said P. J.

Back he turned up the road that led from the sea to the church, and Crotty could do no more but follow him. They hurried along the road past the wood of thorns to the village itself that had a shop and some houses, but not the sign of another soul did they see, and they got to the church where Crotty took a good dab at the holy water. Then they stood under the rope, taking a strong squint at that anchor hung on the cross of the steeple.

'I'll get that,' said P. J. 'I'll get it.'

So they went and opened the door of the steeple and saw a chimney, with a ladder of wood rearing up to the bell-chamber, all covered with barnacles and hairy weeds.

'Go out and hold the rope, Crotty, till I throw the anchor down.' And he did that.

Crotty stood holding the rope amongst the gravestones and they leaning this way and that in the churchyard. There were pools of water round the gravestones and the leaning ones looked as though they were peering down to read their own inscriptions in it. One stone near him gave Crotty a twist of the heart when he had spelled out its words:

Eva
the faithful wife of
Crotty Shinkwin,
sometime of
Ballinarailin.
'Sweet heart of Jesus,
be thou my love.'

He let out a great cry but his comrade did not hear it, for he was crammed in the steeple.

'God rest her soul,' said Crotty, bending over the stone. 'Did a man ever see the like of that! God rest her soul—and soften it, too,' he added. 'Bad it is, for the grass grows on her tomb, and there's muddy water between her and heaven. But good it may be, for the world is made of a roguish nature, and wouldn't it be hard if there was no profit on misfortune at all! I was wearing out my life with both hands, waiting on her tooth and nail, and when I'd a mind to rest she would glare at me with her two cat's eyes!'

He looked round fearfully, as if he might see her tracking him even there. A voice cried: 'Mind yourself, Crotty, she's coming now!' But it was only P. J. pushing his head and arm through a

164

hole in the steeple to take a grab at the anchor. The bell stopped clinking, and down came the anchor at Crotty's feet. Without waiting a moment he heaved it on his shoulder and ran off alone to the boat and cast the anchor aboard. Then he coiled the cable and readied the boat and set the sail. By and by he saw P. J. come stepping along with a bundle under his arm.

'Hurry on,' he shouted, 'hurry now!'

'Be easy, Crotty,' replied his comrade. 'I've the treasure of the world in my arms.'

'What is that, P. J.?'

And P. J. showed him the bundle was a pig's bladder, blown up like a balloon and tied at the throat with a blue ribbon.

''Twas hanging high up in that steeple. 'Tis a bag of air from the garden of Eden itself. A saint brought it away.'

'A saint! What saint?'

'Some holy man, Crotty, but he's gone dead with the hundreds of years.'

'And what's the virtue of it?' Crotty asked.

'Sure,' said P. J., 'and we'd never sink with this aboard. Mind yourself. I'm jumping.'

He took a good leap and landed in the boat. At once there was a terrible scrambling noise in it.

'What! What!' they both cried, stiff with the fear. For the anchor had taken a great jump on to the shore, like a thing alive, it was tearing up the road back to the church, and the rope rushing after as a long snake would.

'It's the anchor!' screamed P. J., and he made a grab at the runaway rope, but as he did so the skin of air from Eden's bower caught in a hooky nail and burst with a noise. Like a big gun, it was. Zip! And P. J. was blown up until he was no bigger than a pin, and then Crotty saw him no more, for the air let out from that bag was like the blast of fifty storms congealed in the crash of one gale. It tore the buttons off his coat and left the roots of thread dangling.

Away rushed the yawl on the crown of the sea, with Crotty alone and the island following him, for the hook was in the steeple again. The wind soon slightened, but Crotty's wits were all scattered and they went journeying upon the waters of the world for two days or three before the gossoon had the sense to cut the rope. And then he cut it. And when he cut it the island stopped, it heaved up in the sea again and turned right over to its own old shape and pattern; the church, the steeple, the pleasant fields, and the wood of thorns, sank in the heart of the ocean and you could see no more than the bare hump of pasture it had always been. The yawl sailed on, and Crotty heard a bird piping. He scanned the sea, and by the safety of God, there was the mainland again, and Ballinarailin again, and Inniskalogue was where it always had been! He set course and—signs on it!—it was not long before he was there where the nuns were bathing, and Tarpy's ass-cart was loading weed.

He fastened up the boat, and he hurried home with the look of decent grief upon him, but by the suit of Satan it was not grief at all when he met Eva Shinkwin at the door, as sleek as an eel, and she glaring at him with her two cat's eyes! It was like the cold nose of a calf pushed in the small of his naked back. He wished he had been able to buy her the makings of a costume, or something.

Where in the name of the king of thunder had he been? Devil and all, what traipsing females had he been after ruining now?

Well, if she *wanted* to know, he could tell her. O yes. Give him a civil word or two, and he would tell her. And it would be the truth. And the whole truth. And nothing but the truth. It would form the formation of all he had to say.

But, holy and sacred medallion, she could never believe a thing like that!

W. B. YEATS

William Butler Yeats was born in Sandymount, County Dublin, Ireland in 1865. He spent his childhood in Country Sligo, and was educated in London, but returned to Dublin at the age of fifteen with the intention of pursuing painting. However, he quickly discovered he preferred poetry, and became involved with the Celtic Revival, an Irish movement resisting the cultural influence of English rule during the Victorian period. Throughout his life, much of Yeats' work was included by Irish mythology and folklore, as well as various types of mysticism and occultism.

Yeats' first verse play, *Mosada*, was published in 1886. Over the next few years, he continued to write, and mingled with many literary luminaries of the day, such as George Bernard Shaw and Oscar Wilde. His *The Wanderings of Usheen and other Poems* was published in 1889, and brought him some attention from critics. In the late 1890s, he became involved with The Abbey Theatre – the institution which propelled him to fame and success. As its chief playwright, Yeats staged a number of his best-remembered productions during the years up to 1911, including *The Countess Cathleen* (1892), *The Land of Heart's Desire* (1894) and *The King's Threshold* (1904).

From 1910 onwards, Yeats focussed more on poetry. The collections of lyrical poetry he penned during his last decades - such as *The Wild Swans at Coole* (1919), *Michael Robartes and the Dancer* (1921), *The Tower* (1928), *The Winding Stair and Other Poems* (1933), and *Last Poems and Plays* (1940) – made him one of the most acclaimed and influential poets in Europe. In 1923, he was awarded the Nobel Prize for Literature. He died in 1939, aged 73, and is now regarded as one of the twentieth century's key English language poets, and a master of the traditional forms.

JAMES STEPHENS

James Stephens was born in Dublin, Ireland in 1882.Over the course of his life, he became famous for his retellings of Irish myths and fairy tales (most notably in his 1920 collection, *Irish Fairy Tales*).Stephens also penned a number of original novels, the most famous of which was probably *Crock of Gold,* and number of anthologies of poetry.During the thirties, Stephens was also an acquaintance of James Joyce.

ELLA YOUNG

Ella Young was born in County Antrim, Ireland in 1867.She received her M.A. from Trinity College, Dublin, and during her studies developed a deep interest in Theosophy.Young was an early member of the Hermetic Society, as well as a devout Irish Republican, even providing armed support to Republican Forces during the Easter Uprising of 1916. Her first volume of verse, simply entitled *Poems,* was published in 1906.Arguably her best-known work, *Celtic Wonder Tales,* appeared four years later.Partly to escape the authorities, Young emigrated to the USA during the twenties, and took up the post of chair in Irish Myth and Lore at the University of California in Berkeley.She lectured widely on topics related to Celtic folklore, while producing a number of well-received works: *The Wonder-Smith and His Son* (1927), *The Tangle-Coated Horse* (1929), and *The Unicorn with Silver Shoes* (1932).In her later years, Young kept an eclectic circle of friends and penned her biography.

DermotO'Byrne (Arnold Bax)

Arnold Edward Trevor Bax – who wrote under the pseudonym Dermot O'Byrne – was born in Streatham, South London, UK in 1883. When he was sixteen, Bax entered the Royal Academy of Music in London, where he excelled at sight-reading and a range of instruments, including piano.Around 1902, he came across the poetry of W. B. Yeats, who became a powerful muse for him.Bax began to develop an infatuation with Ireland, travelling extensively throughout the country and writing many musical works influenced by what he saw.Much of what he produced from 1903 onwards can be seen as a musical counterpart to the Irish Literary Revival.

In 1911, Bax married and settled in Dublin. Here, he began to write poems and short stories, adopting the Celtic pseudonym 'Dermot O'Byrne'.He published a good deal of work, but was perhaps best-known for his flowery poem 'Seafoam and Firelight' (1909).His short stories, most of which depicted everyday life in Ireland, were collected in three collections: *The   Sisters   and   the   Green*

Magic (1912), *Children   of   the   Hills* (1913), and *Wrack* (1918).However, Bax's literary output was forever overshadowed by his musical one, which included seven symphonies, many tone poems, chamber music, concertos, ballets, songs, and choral works.Indeed, he was knighted in 1937, largely for his contributions to music, and became Master of the King's Musick in 1941.

JOSEPH O'NEILL

Joseph O'Neill was born in the Aran Islands, Ireland in 1886.He worked as a school inspector, before becoming Secretary of the Department of Education in the newly formed Irish Free State.Over the course of his life, O'Neill penned five novels, the best-known of which was *Land Under England* (1935), a science-fiction account of a totalitarian society ruled by telepathic mind control.His other works were *Wind From the North* (1934), *Day of Wrath* (1936), *Philip* (1940), *Chosen by the Queen* (1947).

Dorothy Macardle

Dorothy Macardle was born in Dundalk, Ireland in 1889. She attended University College, Dublin, and upon graduating returned to her secondary school to teach English. An active Irish nationalist, Macardle joined a women's paramilitary organisation in 1917, and was arrested during the Irish War of Independence. She recounted her experiences of this time in *Earthbound: Nine Stories of Ireland* (1924), and went on to write a number of plays. In 1937, Macardle published her mammoth work, *The Irish Republic,* now one of the most frequently cited narrative accounts of the Irish War of Independence and its aftermath. She also produced a number of short stories and essays. During the thirties, she worked as a journalist with the League of Nations, and developed a deep concern for the plight of pre-war Czechoslovakia. Macardle was a dedicated political activist right up to her death.

P. W. JOYCE

Patrick Weston Joyce was born in Ballyorgan, Ireland in 1827. He was a native Irish speaker, and began his education at a hedge school before moving to Mitchelstown, County Cork. He went on to gain employment with the Commission of National Education, and completed his education at Trinity College, Dublin. Shortly after graduating, he published, *The Origin and History of Irish Names of Places* (3 volumes; 1869, 1875, 1913), the work for which he remains best-known. Over the rest of his life, he wrote on a wide variety of Irish subjects, from history and folklore to music, and was a key cultural figure of his time. Joyce died in 1914.

JAMES JOYCE

James Joyce was born in Dublin, Ireland in 1882. He excelled as a student at the Jesuit schools Clongowes and Belvedere, and then at University College Dublin, where he studied English, French, and Italian. Upon graduating, Joyce visited Paris, before returning to Dublin due to the death of his mother. In August of 1904, he published his first short story, 'The Sisters,' in the *Irish Homestead Journal.* In October of that same year, he eloped to the continent with his new wife, Nora Barnacle.

The couple spent time in Zurich and Pola (today part of Croatia), before Joyce secured a job teaching English in Trieste, Italy. They remained here for most of the next ten years. Joyce wrote and published articles in Italian in the local newspaper *Piccolo della Sera,* and continued to work on his English-language fiction. 1914 proved an important year for him; *A Portrait of the Artist as a Young Man*, Joyce's first novel, began to appear in serial form in Harriet Weaver's *Egoist*, and his collection of short stories, *Dubliners*, was published. With the onset of World War I, Joyce was able to turn to the novel he had been toying with since 1907: *Ulysses.*

After the war, the modernist poet Ezra Pound persuaded Joyce to come to Paris. His wartime publications had provided him with some fame as an avant-garde writer, as well as a degree of financial security, and he was now able to focus fully on *Ulysses*. Upon its completion, the American journal *The Little Review* began to serialize it, but this came to a halt in 1921 when a court banned the work as obscene. Following a similar reaction in England, Joyce was only able to publish *Ulysses* with the help of Sylvia Beach, an American expatriate living in Paris who owned and ran the bookshop Shakespeare & Co. The novel appeared in February of 1922, and is now regarded as one of the most important works of Modernist literature, and one of the most groundbreaking English language works of all time.

Joyce's last and perhaps most challenging novel, *Finnegans Wake,* was published in 1939. A year later, with the prospect of a Nazi invasion looming, he fled to the south of France, before dying in 1941, at the age of 59.

EIMAR O'DUFFY

Eimar O'Duffy was born in Dublin in 1893. He was
educated at Stonyhurst College, Lancashire, and University
College, Dublin, where he became interested in Irish cultural
and political nationalism. He began publishing in his
twenties, producing his first novel, *The Wasted Island,* in
1919. This early work, which examined critically the origins
of the 1916 Easter Uprising in Ireland, exhibited the sharp
satirical style – and scepticism towards the political direction
of his native country – for which he was to become known.

   Much like other Irish writers such as James Joyce and
Brinsley McNamara, O'Duffy's expression of his
disillusionment with Ireland gained him as many detractors
as it did fans. In 1925, having lost his job at Department of
External Affairs in Dublin as a result of his outspoken views,
he emigrated to England. Here, between 1926 and 1933, he
produced his Cuandine trilogy, the works for which he is

best remembered. A scathing, Swiftian denouncement of the ills of global capitalism and debt culture (O'Duffy was also an astute economist), the trilogy – made up of *King Goshawk and the Birds* (1926), *The Spacious Adventures of the Man in the Street* (1928), and *Asses in Clover (*1933) – is now seen as near-prophetic by some critics, and remains an acclaimed work of satire.

Towards the end of his life, O'Duffy turned his hand to writing detective stories, with mixed success. He also displayed some talent as a literary critic, and was one of the first people to recognize James Joyce's *Ulysses* (1922) as a masterpiece. He died of duodenal ulcers in 1935, at the age of 42.

Lord Dunsany

Lord Dunsany was born Edward John Moreton Drax Plunkett in London in 1878. Dunsany's youth was spent in Dunsany, Ireland – his family home – and Kent. He attended school at Cheam and Eton, before entering the Royal Military Academy Sandhurst in 1896. He inherited his father's title shortly before fighting in the Second Anglo-Boer War between 1899 and 1901. Dunsany published his first book a collection of Anglo-Irish fantasy stories entitled *The Gods of Pegana*, in 1905.

Over the course of his life, Dunsany was a prolific writer, penning short stories, novels, plays, poetry, essays and autobiography. During the peak of his career he was something of a literary celebrity, spending time with authors such as W. B. Yeats and

Rudyard Kipling. He published over sixty books, and his plays were highly successful; at one point, five Dunsany works were running simultaneously in New York. His most notable fantasy short stories were published between 1905 and 1919, in collections such as *The Sword of Welleran and Other Stories* (1908), *A Dreamer's Tales* (1910), *The Book of Wonder* (1912) and *Tales of Wonder* (1916). Amongst his best-regarded novels are *Don Rodriguez: Chronicles of Shadow Valley* (1922), *The King of Elfland's Daughter* (1924), and *The Charwoman's Shadow* (1926).

Dunsany died in old age, following an attack of appendicitis. Over the course of his writing life, he greatly influenced a wide range of authors. Arthur C. Clarke called him "one of the greatest writers of [the 20th] century," and H. P. Lovecraft described him as being "unexcelled in the sorcery of crystalline singing prose, and supreme in the creation of a gorgeous and languorous world of incandescently exotic vision."

A. E. COPPARD

A. E. Coppard was born in Folkestone, England in 1878. Suffering from ill health, he left school at the age of nine and went to work as an assistant to a trouser-maker in Whitechapel, London, during the period of the Jack the Ripper murders. Coppard became a full-time writer in 1919, publishing his first collection of stories, *Adam and Eve and Pinch Me*, in 1921. From this point onwards he was a prolific author of short tales, many of which featured fantastical descriptions of rural England. His most popular collections include *Fishmonger's Fiddle* (1925), *Silver Circus* (1928), *Crotty Shinkwin* (1932), *You Never Know, Do You?* (1939), and *Fearful Pleasures* (1946).

www.ingramcontent.com/pod-product-compliance
Lightning Source LLC
Chambersburg PA
CBHW020658030726
47498CB00002B/564

* 9 7 8 1 4 4 7 4 0 7 1 0 2 *